THE FLOODWOOD CHRONICLES

The Mystery at Owl Canyon

Pete Kennedy

HIGHPOINT
LIT

www.highpointlit.com

The Mystery at Owl Canyon
Copyright © 2025 by Pete Kennedy

This edition published by Highpoint Lit, and imprint of Highpoint Executive Publishing.
For information, write to info@highpointpubs.com.

First Edition
ISBN: 979-8-9989720-2-7

Kennedy, Pete
The Mystery at Owl Canyon

Summary: "In this third volume of Pete Kennedy's Floodwood Chronicles, Professor Artemis Fletcher, artist and adventurer Ayotunde and African fine arts student Olorin travel in 1967 between New York, Mexico City, New Orleans, Rome as they mingle with the greatest female abstract impressionists of the era, face down the power of black magic, and try to prevent the theft of a priceless work of Baroque art. Ultimately a mystical transformation changes the future completely." – Provided by publisher.

ISBN: 979-8-9989720-2-7
(paperback)

Library of Congress Control Number: 2025911410

Cover illustration by Jennifer Lenox, Vermont artist
Design by Sarah M. Clarehart

CONTENTS

PART FOUR   Stealing Strabo

PART FIVE   Passing the Torch

ACKNOWLEDGMENTS

I'd like to thank Maura Kennedy for making this book possible. At Highpoint Lit, thanks to Michael Roney, Sarah Clarehart, Lori Paximadis, and Lauren Fischer. Special thanks to Jennifer Lennox for the cover art.

PROLOGUE
THE SUMMER OF LOVE

You are invited to the Nuptial Celebration of

Dido Anastasia Parren

and

Francis Vincent Faunus

Saturday, June 10, 1967

Lyndhurst Castle

Irvington, New York

Casual wear!

The weather was perfect for a June wedding. Dido looked stunning in her gown, and Faunus was well turned out in a Nehru-style jacket, sandalwood beads, and bell-bottom trousers. To look at him, no one would guess that a year earlier he was a wolf, prowling the hills of Amalfi.

The Sarah Lawrence College contingent—medieval historian Artemis Fletcher, African studies teaching fellow Ayotunde Ibukun, and fine arts student Olorin—were seated together, enjoying the summer sunshine on the sumptuous castle grounds. Artemis raised a can of Tab and proposed a toast.

"May this year prove as interesting as last year, but only in good ways this time!"

"Are you suggesting that being kidnapped and tied to a box of dynamite was interesting, but not in a good way?"

Artemis laughed.

"Tunde, that's exactly what I'm suggesting!"

She took a sip from her can of soda and addressed her colleagues.

"So, what plans do we have for the summer?"

Tunde spoke first.

"Well, I should be working on my book, but what I really want to do is take Olorin here on a road trip. She's been in class since she arrived in the States. Now's her chance to see the country."

"Are you two going out to San Francisco, to put flowers in your hair and join a hippie commune?"

"Not on this trip. You know we're both students of Yoruba culture, and we talked about doing some field research in the Deep South, winding up in New Orleans."

"Olorin, I think Tunde just wants to introduce you to some Louisiana gumbo!"

"That works for me, Artemis! We've talked about the great New Orleans music, too. We both want to research African traditions in the culture down there."

"Well, while you're researching, be cautious. The South can be a dangerous place to just take off down the two-lane highways."

Tunde assumed a cheerfully sarcastic tone.

"Okay, Mom. We'll be careful!"

Tunde popped the top on a can of Fresca.

"How about you, Artemis. Plans?"

"I've got my summer mapped out, and it involves sitting by the pool reading a good book, maybe hitting a few art openings. As a matter of fact, I took the train down into the city yesterday. My old classmate Yoko Ono was staging a 'happening' in a loft down on Chambers Street. Very interesting stuff. Avant-garde. She's been spending a lot of time over in London lately, and she told me she's got a show opening there in the fall. While I was in town, I went to the Strand bookstore and bought Elizabeth Sewell's *The Orphic Voice*. Wasn't her commencement speech on campus just fantastic?"

"Inspiring. Visionary. The way she brings poetry, philosophy, and science together."

"Exactly, Tunde! So, to answer your question, I'm looking forward to a relaxing summer with…"

She glanced around furtively and whispered.

"No extracurricular employment, if you know what I mean."

Tunde laughed.

"Artemis, here comes Kevin Macduff. I have a feeling he might have other ideas for your relaxing summer."

"Artemis, Tunde, Olorin. You look lovely today."

"So do you, Kevin!"

Laughter all around the table.

"I'll take that as a compliment."

The Strabo Society director pulled up a folding chair.

"Artemis, this castle is pretty amazing."

"I'm glad you like it, Kevin. I had to break my piggy bank to buy it."

"On a schoolteacher's salary? I'm not gonna fall for that!"

"Actually, it belonged to Jay Gould, one of those robber barons. It's an event space now."

"Well, it's a little bit more impressive than my studio apartment in the Bronx."

Macduff pulled his chair closer and lowered his voice.

"Artemis, I got a call this morning at the club. I need you for a mission. How does Mexico sound?"

"If the mission is lying on the beach at Veracruz, it sounds pretty darn good."

"I'm afraid that's not quite it, but it's an interesting assignment: art, culture, maybe even a little witchcraft."

"Hmm, now there's a trifecta. Okay, when do I fly out?"

"Sunday the eighteenth, a week from tomorrow. I'll fill you in on the details when I get back to the office on Monday."

"Got it, Kevin. And by the way, may I remind you that we're not in the office right now?" Artemis gave a sweeping gesture. "We're at a beautiful castle on the Hudson, our friends just got married, and it's a gorgeous day."

In the big tent, the Lovin' Spoonful started tuning up.

"So, let's all get in there and do some dancing!"

PART ONE

THE
CURANDERA

CHAPTER 1

THE ASSIGNMENT

Monday, June 12, 1967
New York City

Artemis and Macduff grabbed a booth at the Carnegie Deli.

"Tuna melt and coffee, please."

"Cheeseburger and a Coke."

"So Kevin, what's up in Mexico?"

"An art opening in Mexico City, at the Galería de Arte Mexicano. The gallery director, Ines Amor, is a champion of Surrealist art, and she's planning a gala opening a week from today featuring several women who've formed an interesting community of painters, sculptors, photographers, and authors in the city."

"Sounds like something that I'd like to attend, even if it wasn't an assignment."

"It gets more interesting. Several of the women who are active in the community came to Mexico as political exiles, fleeing the Nazis in Europe. The Mexican government welcomed refugees during the lead up to World War II, so the arts community is made up of creative people from England, Spain, and France as well as Mexican-born artists."

"Kevin, you've referred to the Surrealist artists twice specifically as women. Was that deliberate?"

"It was indeed. Indulge me, Artemis, for a bit of quick history. Surrealism looks to unite the conscious mind with the unconscious, the waking world with the dreamworld. It became a movement in Paris in the 1920s where there was a growing interest in the psychology of Carl Jung. Salvador Dalí and Max Ernst were early pioneers of the genre."

"You forgot André Breton. I'm a history professor, Kevin, remember? But I'm intrigued by one thing. The Surrealist movement was founded by men in Paris, but the exhibit we're talking about is by women in Mexico City, who came over from Europe. There's a *vive la différence* going on here. What's up with the gender disparity?"

"That's a key point, Professor Fletcher. The Parisian Surrealists were men who took lovers, oftentimes women who were talented artists in their own right. They kept them in the role of muses, inspiring sort of fairy children, connected with the mystic world of the unconscious. That would be all well and good, except that there was an informal, unspoken sort of taboo on the women becoming equal partners in the creative movement. If they were talented, that was to be kept under wraps."

"That wouldn't sit well with me!"

"It didn't sit well with the women artists, either. The artists featured in the upcoming exhibit include several women who fled Europe during the war years, and when they settled and joined their creative forces in Mexico City, they found that they were liberated to follow their own feminine-based inspiration instead of playing the role of someone else's muse."

"Speaking of roles, what exactly is my role at this new exhibition?"

Macduff sipped his soda.

"Artemis, we're both aware of the protests going on here in the States."

"Over the slow implementation of the Civil Rights Act."

"Correct. There's real fear that violence could erupt here in the States this summer. Well, Mexico is going through a similar period of unrest, with students at the forefront. There are calls for income equality in Mexico City, where preparations are being made for the Olympics next year. People are calling for that money to be spent instead on improving social conditions. Clearly, we have no jurisdiction there, but in the interest of preserving and furthering the arts scene, it's imperative for Strabo to have someone on the ground keeping an eye on the developing situation. This Surrealist art exhibit could be a flash point, and we need an agent with experience and a cool head to focus on the safety of the art and the artists, without getting involved in the politics. That person would be you."

"So, my mission is to do nothing but enjoy the art, but keeping my antennae tuned for any trouble."

"Well, you've got to admit that you have a sixth sense for that sort of thing."

"You got it, Kevin. If I don't find trouble, it finds me."

"That's why we love you, Artemis!"

Macduff laid a manila envelope on the table.

"Your flight info for Sunday morning and a ticket to Miami, connecting through on Mexicana Air, are in this packet, along with the information for your contact in Mexico City. She is a friend of the society, and as a matter of fact, she's one of the artists in the exhibit. *Buen viaje!*"

CHAPTER 2

THE MEXICAN CONNECTION

Sunday, June 18, 1967
Mexico City

"*Hola*, Artemis! *Como estás?*"

The enthusiastic greeting came from an effervescent figure straight out of a Carnaby Street fashion spread. Viviana Villalobos wore a paisley minidress and white tights. Her hair was long and straight, with bangs that nearly covered her dark brown eyes. She introduced herself with a vigorous handshake that roused Artemis from her long-flight torpor.

"Viviana Villalobos. What a lovely name."

"That's me. The vivacious wolf!"

She laughed and embraced Artemis as if they were long-lost friends.

"Kevin informed me by telegram that you have no checked baggage, so grab your duffel bag and let's get moving pronto. We've got shopping to do, *amiga!*"

Viviana skillfully negotiated the dense traffic leaving the airport and turned west toward the city center.

"Artemis, you might find the Mercado Sonora just a bit overwhelming. It's *muy grande.*"

"I've found my way in and out of the old Straw Market in Nassau."

"Well, multiply that by a power of ten! Just follow along with me. The vendors establish neighborhoods, so to speak, and it helps to know the lay of the land in advance. I grew up here in Ciudad de Mexico, so I will be your expert tour guide."

A small city of tent-covered vendor booths surrounded a complex of seven massive Quonset huts, each one large enough to house a jet airliner. As they made their way through the labyrinth of shouting vendors, Artemis, ever the historian, wondered if the same site had been a marketplace stretching back into prehistory, when the ancient Aztec capital was situated here, on an island in the middle of a long-gone lake.

"Tell me Artemis, are you an animal lover?"

"Well, I was a champion crossbow archer when I was young. That involved hunting, and eventually I was sickened by the cruelty. I stuck with the archery, but nowadays I mostly aim at targets stuffed with straw."

She chuckled, thinking back to the temple in Kyoto.

"And the occasional criminal."

"Okay then, I share your love for animals, so there are certain precincts inside the *mercado* that we will not visit. Enough said about that?"

"*Sí, de hecho.* Yes indeed!"

"Now, I don't come here to shop for groceries. I come for *brujería*, magic. I am a *curandera.*"

"And that is…?"

"A practitioner of traditional medicine. Many of our customs here in Mexico are blended with ancient knowledge handed down from the Oto people, long before the Aztecs. Then we mix in Aztec history, the Spanish Catholic overlay, and modern-day science, medicine, philosophy, and so on. It's a *guiso* that suits our temperament. We're always looking forward, but also always staying in contact with our history, our deepest roots. A *curandera* is a sort of healer."

"Maybe I'm just thinking like a twentieth-century American here, but don't you get pushback from the medical industry?"

"The pushback started long before the twentieth century, Artemis! You're a medieval scholar, is that correct?"

"That's correct, when I'm not wandering around vast, exotic marketplaces."

"No doubt you've heard of the *Malleus Maleficarum*."

"Fourteen eighty-six. I test my freshman students on the date."

"Then you know that it was a handbook for identifying witches, and a witch was any woman who dared to step outside the role of homemaker, especially women who were skilled in professions that men saw as their exclusive province. That could be any skill that might enable them to achieve financial independence and success. *Ay caramba*, did they find a lot of witches, including in your Salem trials in New England. Here in Mexico, the old term they used was *endemoniado*, possessed by a demon, or *endiablado*, possessed by the devil. It would have been simpler just to say they were guilty of competing with men in the professions."

They stopped at a stand selling soda pop and bought two tamarind Jarritos. The vendor tried to entice them with a bottle of Aguascalientes agave-flavored tequila, but Viviana waved him off.

"It's a little early in *el dia, señor*!"

In the multiodiferous shade of the huge building, they were looking down a long central passage, like standing at the narthex of a strange, chaotic cathedral.

"Tomorrow, Artemis, we'll view artworks by three women who brazenly, and with great good humor, called themselves the three witches. But for now, let's explore the *mercado*."

"Three witches! I do hope Macbeth makes an appearance. Lead on, Viviana!"

They snaked their way through the throngs to the herb vendors. Viviana kept a running commentary on the various ingredients and what types of maladies they might treat.

"I'm curious. What kind of therapy do you practice, Viviana?"

"Dreams, Artemis. Dreams that connect you to the unconscious. That's the essence of Surrealism. This Friday is the end of the full moon. It's also Saint John's Eve. That's a night rich with dreams. I know they are coming, so I am preparing myself by being here in the *mercado*, a place of magic. Let's take a look at these charms."

They came to a booth that featured religious statuettes and other talismans.

"Viviana, isn't that Saint Teresa of Avila?"

"Oh yes, our beloved Teresa. We often invoke her in a magical way. For one thing, she was Spanish, an ancestor, but more to the point, she was a mystic. She was a visionary, living on the border of dreaming and waking. Here in Mexico, we value that kind of personality. It fits our character, our culture. She was also attacked because she stepped out of the cloister and acted on her faith, drawn from her own mystical experiences, rather than just following dogma handed down by the church fathers. Do you see why the women Surrealists here in Mexico honor her? She embodies our spirit of independence and our belief in a personal vision quest."

She scanned a table of various powders in plastic bags.

"These are *remedios* that cross over into the realm of *brujería*, magic. Salt from the ocean is tossed into the air to dispel what the old ones would call evil spirits. Dust from the magic regions of Mexico is scattered, and *curanderas* sometimes rub ash from sacred mountains between their palms before they perform healing rituals."

She stopped to examine a ceramic skull.

"Artemis, in your country this skull, which we call a *calavera*, would be a prop in a horror film, but here in Mexico it is part of our celebration of the ancestors. Being ancestors, they are no longer alive, so the day we celebrate them is our Dia de los Muertos, the Day of the Dead. It's your All Saints' Day, the day after Halloween. It's fitting to celebrate those who came before, and rather than be frightened of them, we treat them like the family that they are. Here, take a look at this."

An artist was finishing off a wood carving of a whimsical Ford convertible, occupied by a smiling family of skeletons. A surfboard extended from the trunk.

"I think they are heading for the beach, Artemis! Our *alibrijes* figures, as we call them, range from the spiritual to the downright silly. We honor our ancestors, and that includes having fun with them."

Viviana made her purchases and pointed down the long aisle toward the outside world.

"Artemis, I think it's time we got you some home-cooked *comida* and a good night's rest. We have a big day *mañana*!"

CHAPTER 3

THE DREAM

Artemis kept her eyes closed as Viviana maneuvered her tiny VW through the high-speed traffic across town. The bug, painted roof-to-floorboards with sunflowers, finally came to rest on a quiet residential side street.

"Artemis, this is Colonia Roma del Norte. It's one of two neighborhoods here on the west side of center city where artists have gathered for decades. Perhaps it's like your Greenwich Village. Inexpensive rent and small dwellings, but that's okay, because we gather in the coffee shops. Poets, painters, and musicians share ideas. There's an element of traditional Mexican art in the air, but so many émigrés gather here that there's oftentimes a feeling that one is in Europe, perhaps in the café culture of Montmartre. Here's my place. I hope you don't mind walking up a few flights!"

Viviana's top-floor garret consisted of just two rooms. Late-afternoon sun streamed through a skylight, illuminating a painter's studio cluttered with canvases, jars of paint, and buckets of brushes. The carpet was a paint-splattered canvas tarpaulin that resembled the work of Jackson Pollock. In the brightest sunlit corner, an easel supported Viviana's current work in progress, a hybrid of traditional Mexican animal figures mixed with elements of abstract expressionism. Record albums haphazardly lined the floorboards. Beneath the only street-facing window was the sink, a small refrigerator, and a two-burner hot plate. A brightly striped serape hung over an old-fashioned couch that looked like it had been rescued from a tag sale. The only other furnishings were two kitchen chairs and a small Formica-topped table, with a wine bottle dripping with candle wax for the centerpiece. A door, draped with another serape, led to an inner sanctum where Viviana presumably slept and practiced her *curandera* magic.

Over bowls of rice, black beans, and *pico de gallo* washed down by candlelight with cups of home-brewed tea, the two women bonded over their mutual love for modern jazz, especially Charles Mingus and Thelonious Monk, although Artemis was forced to confess her ignorance concerning the minutiae of the Beatles' album repertoire.

"Artemis, you must promise you'll come down again for a visit, and I'll play them all for you, right up to *Sgt. Pepper's Lonely Hearts Club Band*, the one that just came out!"

The promise procured, Viviana blew out the candle and retired to the bedroom. On the humble old couch, Artemis felt like she was in the lap of luxury after a long day that began in New York and ended with a treatise on magical healing in Mexico. She fell at once into a deep sleep.

Artemis dreamed that she was becoming smaller and smaller. She became so small that she dispersed into separate cells, and then the cells broke down into atoms, and the atoms simplified into the primary colors. She became liquid: red, blue, and yellow. She was not afraid, but she had a sense that she would need a painter to reconstitute her. Things progressed rapidly, as they do in dreams, and soon she was being pumped out of three tubes, one for each color, onto an easel. It was a way of being born. Before long, a paintbrush mixed her into shades of brown, the combination of all three colors, and she was painted onto a canvas. She didn't remain flat for very long. In fact, in no time at all she rose up, spread wings, and flew straight out the window of a tall medieval tower. She felt free, flying, untethered to the earth. Reborn.

CHAPTER 4

THE PAINTING

Monday, June 19, 1967
Mexico City

Artemis woke to the smell of ground beans percolating in a tin pot on the hot plate. She felt refreshed and anxious to get on with her assignment. She looked forward to guarding the exhibit, but now she was drawn to the paintings. She felt that the dream was guiding her there, that there was something important for her to see.

Over cups of strong Mexican coffee laced with cocoa and cinnamon, Viviana laid out the day's agenda.

"On our way over to the gallery, I'm going to take a quick detour a few blocks north of Avenida Hidalgo to show you Calle Gabino Barreda. It's a street in Colonia San Rafael, the other neighborhood that, like this one, was a haven for the Surrealist artists. Number 18 Gabino Barreda was the home of Remedios Varo. She was born in Spain but made a dramatic escape from Europe by way of Casablanca, just like in the movie! Artemis, do you remember when I mentioned the three witches yesterday at the *mercado*?"

"Oh yes, and I pictured the opening of *Macbeth*!"

"Well, shift the scene of your drama from Scotland to Mexico. Remedios and her fellow artists Leonora Carrington and Kati Horna liked to call themselves the three witches. They were interested in all kinds of magic and esoterica, and they pursued a creative path that supposedly excluded women. Witches, indeed!"

Viviana drained her coffee cup and sighed reflectively.

"We lost Remedios just a few years ago, but through her work, she will be very much present today at the exhibit. You'll see. Then we'll go to the gallery, where I'll introduce you to Ines Amor, the gallery director. She's the hub of Mexico City's art world. But first I must ask you a question, *mi amiga*."

"Of course."

Artemis put her cup down on the saucer.

"Do you recall that yesterday I referred to myself as the wolf?"

"Oh yes. The vivacious wolf!"

"Tell me, did you think I was speaking metaphorically or literally?"

"Well, now that you ask, I don't know. I didn't give it much thought at all."

"You fly home tomorrow, Tuesday. Is that correct?"

"Yes, back to New York to work on a book."

"And the moon is not full until Thursday, so…"

Viviana took a sip from her coffee cup and smiled slyly.

"I guess we'll never know for sure, will we?"

Before Artemis had a chance to decide whether her hostess had just shared a sisterly secret, the spell was broken.

"We need to *vamos* if we want to make it to the opening on time!"

As she negotiated the traffic crawling north on Avenida Insurgentes, Viviana filled in bits of history for Artemis.

"San Rafael, the neighborhood we'll detour through on the way to the gallery, was a gathering place for artists starting back during World War II, when Europe was experiencing the exodus of intellectuals and creative types. Calle Gabino Barreda, where Remedios lived, was the central street of the San Rafael arts community."

She turned off the main artery and began skillfully wending through residential streets.

"Some of the artists who lived and worked here are no longer living, but their work will be living today in the gallery. Isn't that a wonderful thing about art, Artemis? It's timeless, whereas our bodies have a deadline that we can only delay, but we cannot avoid."

"I'm eager to see the paintings now that I have a sense of place and a feel for the community of women who created them."

"*Sí, de hecho*. But enough tourism! You have an assignment to guard an exhibit, and I have paintings to display. *Vamos!*"

At the Galería de Arte Mexicano, the two women were greeted just inside the doors by Ines Amor. As director of the gallery, curator of the permanent collection, and tireless promotor of Mexican art, she was the guiding force of the contemporary movement.

"Viviana, you look lovely, as always, and vivacious as well, I might add."

She turned to Artemis.

"The Strabo Society has been a valuable partner in our effort to encourage creativity here in Ciudad de México. Your presence adds an extra note of *gracia* to the opening today. Now, I must continue to meet and greet. Please enjoy your exploration of the galleries before our invited guests arrive."

Viviana acted as tour guide.

"Do not miss the Frida Kahlo gallery, but let's visit the Carrington exhibit first. Leonora was born to a wealthy family in England. Her father was a merchant who strongly desired for her to marry into the nobility. She was a rebellious, creative child who had other ideas. Just out of her teens, she ran off to Paris and joined the Surrealist circle there. As World War II approached, the next few years were a series of harrowing escapes, until she found a permanent home here in Mexico City. Her art is mystical, with a visionary language of its own, but her symbols are deeply resonant. Here we are."

The paintings were replete with dream imagery. Hooded figures, horses, and fantastical creatures seemed to be involved in healing, caregiving rituals. Medieval elements, using egg tempera like the old icons, suggested a kind of sacramental reverence, but in a surreal setting. Some of them made reference to Celtic lore, tracing back to Carrington's Irish mother. All in all, there was something consoling, something nurturing, in the strange characters and settings. Everything seemed unique and otherworldly and yet not unsettling, emerging from some comforting region of the subconscious. Artemis felt bathed in a sort of blissful light.

"Next is the Remedios Varo exhibit. Artemis, you must go there on your own. I am on duty, so to speak, in my own gallery, greeting visitors. Let's reconvene at the end of the day and get some rest back at *mi casa* before you fly out in the morning."

Artemis walked into the next gallery and nearly collapsed. She stood frozen, staring at the canvas in the center of the wall in front of her. She sat on a padded bench facing the painting and composed herself, taking long, deep breaths. The dizziness subsided, and she began absorbing the details of the painting. The title plaque read *Creation of the Birds*, and below that, *Remedios Varo, 1957*. The setting was a tower with small corner buttresses that suggested the Middle Ages. An artist was seated at a desk. She had a woman's hands, feet, and smiling mouth, but her body was covered with feathers. She gazed down at her work with the enormous eyes of an owl. Next to her desk, a strange kind of pump was dispensing the three primary colors onto an easel. In the center of the easel, the artist had mixed them together into a brown earth tone. Around the artist's neck hung a small guitar, and one string of the guitar extended down to the canvas on the desk, ending as a fine paintbrush. As she painted with her right hand, she held a triangular magnifying glass aloft in her left, at such an angle that it caught and refracted the rays of the distant moon, as they shone through a tower window. The owl was more than an artist; she was a magician, for as each picture was completed and caught the moonlight, it turned into a live bird that spread its wings and flew out the window into the moonlit night.

Artemis knew the painting. She had seen it in the dreamworld only hours before. Never having heard of Remedios Varo, she knew nonetheless that back when she woke up something, or someone, had summoned her all the way from Valhalla, New York, for this moment, to see this depiction of her dream, the dream where she was the paint, she was the painting, and she was the newborn bird who flew off into the night. What it meant, she didn't know yet, but she felt an immense calm, a feeling that she was surrounded by nourishing entities who cared for her. Since her own mother had died in childbirth, it was the first time in her life that she had known that feeling.

On the ride home, Artemis was silent, turning over the dream image in her head. The usually gregarious Viviana was silent as well, letting her companion process what she had seen and felt at the gallery.

Over a candlelit dinner of leftover rice and beans, the mystery was finally addressed.

"Artemis, the occasional work that I do for the Strabo Society is mundane. Sometimes it's cops and robbers; other times it's more enjoyable, like this assignment: spending time with you. That's not my real occupation, though. I told you that I am a *curandera*, a healer. My special power is *sueños*, the ability to harness dreams and bring them to life: my life, and the lives of others. This is not something one can learn in a school. I was blessed by the old ones while still in my mother's womb, and they began teaching me before I could talk. Later, when they died, they passed into me, and they still teach and guide me. That's the real meaning of Dia de los Muertes. The ancestors live within us. Just think, Artemis, you and I both have skeletons under our skin!"

She laughed at the image.

"They often counsel me in dreams, and I have learned to counsel others in their dreams."

Artemis asked a direct question.

"Are you one of the old ones?"

"If I answer that, it will create a distance. I would become a mysterious entity to you. I prefer that we remain *hermanas*, sisters."

She closed her eyes and sighed.

"Artemis, I am in no way a fortune teller, but I can use my *sueños* power, the dream power, to help others see their own path."

"Are you talking about *Creation of the Birds*?"

"Let me tell you, the Surrealist artists here in Mexico City are healers themselves. Women of power, nurturing power. They believe that if there are gods, they are more likely to be birds than superhumans. That's all right there in the painting."

"And it's all in the dream I had the night before I even saw the painting. So, you planted the dream?"

"Artemis, because your mother died giving birth to you, you never knew her. Your father trained you to have steely-eyed focus, to extinguish self-doubt, to be always on target. You have lived your life as Cleopatra."

"Cleopatra! How is that?"

"Her name was Greek. *Cleo* means 'honor' and *patra* means 'father.' 'Honor the father.' You've honored your father, Alcon, by living his ideals in a life of service. The dream means that you have *done* that, and now you're ready to fly to what comes next. That's the reason you came to Mexico, to dream that dream and see the painting. You were sent here not just by Kevin Macduff but by someone more powerful, someone watching over you: your mother. I'm just the intermediary."

She picked up the empty wine bottle that served as a candle holder.

"I'm going to my own dreamworld now. Coffee in the morning?"

"*Sí.* Thanks for everything, Viviana."

"*Dulces sueños*, Artemis!"

As midnight passed and the taxi horns of Colonia Roma del Norte fell silent, Artemis had another dream in which she was watching an artist at work. This time, it was an old woman in Navajo dress. She was bent over a sand painting. She was carefully touching vegetable tinctures on the ground and transferring them onto the work in progress. A single shaft of moonlight was illuminating the scene, streaming down from a thin crevice in the ceiling of what appeared to be a narrow cave. Artemis felt herself become weightless. She floated above the old woman, toward the crevice. Just before she wafted into the open air, she glanced down and saw that the woman was working on a partially completed icon of a bird: a great horned owl. As Artemis drifted up toward the dream sky, a car horn beeped on the *calle* below the apartment window, and she woke with a start. She glanced around and realized she was lying on Viviana's couch, covered by her hostess's woven agave serape. She fell back into a deep sleep.

CHAPTER 5

DEPARTURE

Tuesday, June 20, 1967
Mexico City to New York City

At the Mexicana Air departure gate, Viviana embraced Artemis again and gave her a kiss on the cheek, as *las hermanas* do in Mexico.

"Safe travels, sister! And one more thing."

She leaned in.

"When I called myself the wolf, I was being literal, not metaphorical. You must come down sometime on the full moon and we will travel to Las Pozas, the Surrealist valley in the northern mountains. That's where I sequester. There will be another time, Artemis. We will meet again. *Buen viaje*!"

Artemis boarded the 727 for home. She was a bit shaken by her forty-eight hours in Mexico. For the first time, she felt mothered. By a painting and a dream in which she dissolved and was reborn to spread new wings. For the first time, she felt that perhaps she didn't need to stand alone like Joan of Arc against the forces of evil. Perhaps she had done her work.

As her connecting flight departed from Miami, she recalled that Ayotunde and Olorin had talked about a road trip in the Jeep. They were heading all the way down south to New Orleans, sticking to the back roads. That sounded to Artemis like a trip tailor-made for a couple of intrepid youngsters, and there would no doubt be tales told about their adventures when the team reconvened next week in Valhalla.

PART TWO

The Eve of Saint John

CHAPTER 6

ROAD TRIP!

Sunday June 18, 1967
New York City to Asbury Park, New Jersey

On the crowded drop-off ramp at JFK, Tunde and Olorin wished Artemis a safe journey to Mexico, while cabs honked impatiently behind them. The Jeep pulled away from the departure area and crawled slowly in a caravan of traffic on the Van Wyck Expressway.

"Expressway. Bit of an ironic name, I would say."

"That's okay, Tunde. I'm using the time to study this road atlas. I want to have a mental picture of our route, as if I'm looking down from the sky."

"The sky would be quicker, but we'd miss so much. We're going to stay on the two-lane roads and see America down here on the ground. Here's what I'm thinking. We drive down to Asbury Park on the Jersey Shore tonight. We can check out some music there and stay over. Tomorrow, we continue down the shore and ride the Cape May ferry over to Delaware. Then we'll make our way to Washington and spend the night. In the morning we'll take off for the South. I'm thinking Memphis next, and then down through Mississippi to the Big Easy."

"The Big Easy?"

"That's just one of the names for New Orleans. How does that all sound?"

"It sounds like a road trip to me!"

Traffic eased as they traveled south on the Jersey Turnpike and the city skyline grew smaller in the rearview mirror. The Garden State Parkway and Route 33 brought them into Asbury Park. Olorin was excited.

"Let's drive along the beach!"

Tunde navigated down Kingsley Street, parallel to the ocean. The boardwalk was anchored by the massive Convention Hall. Olorin pointed at a billboard.

COMING JULY 1

RAY CHARLES

"Oh my gosh, Tunde. Ray Charles! Everyone back home knows 'What'd I Say'!"

At the end of Kingsley Street, they jogged onto Lake Avenue, wending their way to Springwood Avenue, the main street of Asbury Park's West Side neighborhood.

Springwood was a classic main drag, a forum where neighbors gathered at barber shops, beauty parlors, and butcher shops during the day, and bars, restaurants, and nightclubs by night. The top names in jazz and soul music came through town, performing at venues that were packed on weekends. Olorin read off the names of businesses as Tunde motored west on the avenue:

SOPHIE'S SHOES

PERELLA'S MEAT MARKET

KNUCKLE'S ELECTRIC
MILLER'S CHICKEN MART
SCALPATI THE SHOEMAKER

A neon sign lit up the corner of Springwood and Atkins.

MICKEY'S TRACKSIDE CLUB

The club's marquee read:

TONIGHT: CEE CEE HARRIS AND THE DUKES OF RHYTHM

Tunde parked under the neon sign, and they entered. It was an elegant space. A crystal chandelier hung above the small stage. A woman in a satin gown was playing a big Hammond organ. Her long fingers were laden with jeweled rings, but that didn't seem to slow her down as she improvised chords and melodies. The organ seemed to sing an old, sad song of mystery, a song sung by someone far from home. Olorin and Tunde listened, transfixed. When the musicians took a break, the woman sat right down at their table.

"Now, where are y'all from?"

"Valhalla, New York. Well, I'm originally from Scarsdale," Tunde said.

"And I'm from Osogbo, Nigeria," Olorin said.

"Nigeria!"

Miss Harris smiled playfully.

"And you came all the way to Springwood Avenue just to hear us play!"

"Oh, it's an honor, ma'am," Olorin said.

"You came on a good night. This place is jumpin' on weekends, but on Sunday business is slow, and I can play whatever I want. If you'd come down Springwood Avenue early this morning, you could have heard me just down the block, playing at the Baptist church. Oh, I keep busy!"

Miss Harris thanked the women for coming as the musicians gathered back on the bandstand. Tunde and Olorin thanked her in turn for the music. Exhausted from the day's drive, they decided to skip the second show, so they left the Jeep where it was parked and checked in next door to the club at Mrs. Burgess's Metropolitan Hotel to get some sleep. They had many miles to travel.

CHAPTER 7

JUNETEENTH

Monday, June 19, 1967
Asbury Park, New Jersey, to Washington, DC

In the morning they strolled down the avenue to Chet's Grill. Over a hearty breakfast of pan-fried green tomatoes, slow-cooked greens, and sauteed okra, they discussed the day's itinerary.

"Olorin, do you know what day this is?"

"Monday?"

"Well, yes. But it's a special Monday. It's June 19. Juneteenth!"

"Tell me about Juneteenth, Tunde."

"I'll give you a chronology, and that will explain the significance. Ready?"

Olorin took a sip of coffee.

"A chronology. Okay, Tunde. Hit me with some dates!"

"Here we go. In the 1860s, the Civil War was raging over whether newly admitted states would be allowed to continue the tragedy of slavery. On January 1, 1863, President Lincoln issued the Emancipation Proclamation, declaring all slaves in America free. It wasn't a law yet, so he had to persuade Congress to vote for a constitutional amendment that would officially ban slavery. It took two years to do that. The amendment was finally ratified on January 31, 1865. Needless to say, Olorin, newspapers in the Confederate states didn't rush to announce the news. It was only after the South surrendered on April 9 that Union troops were able to start spreading the word as they moved through the region. It took over two months for them to reach the furthest outpost of slavery: Galveston, Texas. That day, June 19, is celebrated as our own special Independence Day, the last day of legal slavery."

"Tunde, I wonder how many of my own ancestors, kidnapped from my homeland, celebrated on that day."

"The struggle goes on, Olorin. Dr. King has a new book, titled *Where Do We Go from Here?* He's been talking about the aftermath of the Civil Rights Act that was passed three years ago, and how there's so much impatience to achieve equality. It's been such a long struggle. Dr. King has been cautioning about violence, warning about what he calls the 'long hot summer' this year."

"Tunde, growing up in Osogbo, surrounded by forest, where there are all kinds of dangers, I learned that fear is a valuable sense that we must pay attention to. I feel it here now, on Springbrook Avenue. I've been reading about that long hot summer idea in the *Times* this morning. Just in the last week, riots in Cincinnati, Philadelphia, Los Angeles. And now there's trouble in Atlanta, too. On top of it all, there's talk of a coming civil war in my home country. I fear for my mother, and for the sacred grove."

Tunde took a sip from her coffee cup. "Olorin, you and I live under a protective shield, don't we? At Artemis's beautiful estate, and on the campus of a liberal college. It's a good thing for us to get out here in the real world, but it's just so hard to understand the prejudice. Even here, enjoying Springwood Avenue, we're still across the tracks from the resort world of Asbury Park, cut off from the boardwalk and the beach. Why do the roots of segregation run so deep? I just hope we can cling to Dr. King's message of nonviolence this summer. Did you read in the *Times* about that big rock music festival out in California over the weekend? Maybe the hippies are onto something."

They sat silently for a few moments. Then, Tunde drained her coffee cup and put a five-dollar bill on the counter.

"Let's gas up the Jeep and hit the road."

The cruise down Highway 9 to Cape May was relaxing, and the ferry trip across Delaware Bay was even more so. The pastures and cornfields of Maryland's Eastern Shore seemed a world apart from the America across Chesapeake Bay. Broad creeks crisscrossed the peninsula. Tunde wondered which one was the route that Frederick Douglass took on his flight to freedom. It was a secret he never revealed, since that would have jeopardized others who followed in his footsteps to freedom. Juneteenth was a thought-provoking day to be traveling through former slave lands.

After a bumper-to-bumper trip across the two-lane Chesapeake Bay bridge, they passed the colonial-style buildings of the Naval Academy in Annapolis and made their way into the Washington, DC, suburbs. Ayotunde had been there once on a high school social studies trip.

"Let's take a quick auto tour around the landmarks, and then hit a few high points."

Olorin surveyed the area around the national mall with interest.

"Tunde, I'm looking at these white marble domes and pillars, and that huge obelisk. You know what it brings to mind?"

"Let me guess. Ancient Rome?"

"Exactly!"

"Well, that's probably what the urban designers had in mind, but let's head uptown to some sights that are not quite as grandiose, but they have their own kind of history."

Tunde navigated the traffic up 14th Street to U Street.

"U Street. This was called Black Broadway back in the old days. Like Harlem, it's been a center of the arts, culture, and learning for decades. Howard University, Griffith Stadium, the Howard Theatre—there are so many landmarks in this neighborhood. Over there is the Lincoln Theatre. Look at the marquee, Olorin! Duke Ellington's coming. He grew up right around the corner."

"Tunde, this is amazing!"

"Well, now that we've seen Black Broadway, the White House, the Capitol, and the Washington Monument, let me show you my personal favorite DC landmark. I hope you're hungry."

She found a parking spot right in front of Ben's Chili Bowl.

"You haven't lived until you've had a Ben's half-smoke!"

They feasted on massive hot dogs, smothered in onions and chili. They washed the high-calorie cornucopia down with chocolate milkshakes.

"Olorin, I must be a bad influence on the young. That was utterly decadent!"

Olorin laughed.

"If that's decadence, keep it coming!"

"Let's grab a room down the block at the Whitelaw and get some rest. We've got a long drive tomorrow."

CHAPTER 8

OLORIN'S LESSON

Tuesday, June 20, 1967
Washington, DC, to Memphis, Tennessee

It was a relief to break free from the increasing glut of traffic on the recently constructed Capital Beltway at dawn. Tunde relaxed as they motored down Highway 29 into Virginia, hooking up with Interstate 66. The landscape opened out to rolling hills. At Strasburg they connected with Interstate 81 and began the trip down the Shenandoah Valley. The rounded Blue Ridge Mountains rose gently to the east and west, enclosing a bucolic landscape of dairy farms and fields of growing spring wheat.

Feeling creative, the explorers stopped at a farmstand near Luray and bought sachets of mountain laurel for a bit of interior decoration in the Jeep. The road rose into the Great Smoky highlands when they passed Galax and crossed into Tennessee. As they made the turn westward from I-81 onto I-40, Olorin glanced up at a passenger jet, thirty thousand feet above them, heading north.

"You know, Tunde, that could be Artemis. Isn't she flying home from Mexico today?"

"You just might be right, Olorin. Hard to tell from down here!"

Tunde thought back to her early trips with Artemis. She was the protégé then, and Artemis was the veteran mentor. Now, she was the veteran and Olorin was her protégé. She had a feeling that her Nigerian-born traveling companion had a store of power that transcended her skill as an artist. There was a magical aura around her, and Tunde was looking forward to seeing how it might play out, should circumstances require, on their road adventure.

They bypassed Knoxville, crossed the high Cumberland Plateau, and descended into the broad central valley of Tennessee, crisscrossing the winding Harpeth and Caney Fork Rivers as they headed straight west. When they reached Nashville, they stopped to gas up again.

Demonbreun Street, just off the interstate, was a row of glitzy faux-Western shops. The two travelers, looking for a break from the road, decided to peruse the offerings. Gaudy rhine-stone-studded shirts, outsized cowboy hats, and unplayable plastic guitars lured tourists into the mercantile world of country music. The women smiled and raised eyebrows at the garish merchandise, but Olorin's brow crinkled when they came upon a shelf of "mammy" dolls, cheap stuffed figurines depicting the slave women who kept house and raised the master's children. She was taken aback that toys celebrating slavery were for still on sale, after the years of civil rights struggle in America had supposedly mitigated the arrogance of openly displayed racism.

Tunde could see Olorin's distress. She shared it, although she wasn't taken by surprise. She knew to keep silent in the store, so she raised an eyebrow and nodded toward the exit.

As the Jeep pulled back onto the highway heading west, she broached the subject.

"Olorin, I'm sorry you had to see those dolls. I should have warned you."

She was quiet for a moment, choosing her words.

"It was me who suggested we take a road trip across America. That's a great thing for you, having moved here so recently from Nigeria, isn't it? I will confess that I planned our route to travel deep into the South, the part of this country that seceded over the issue of slavery. It's part of our national history, and we need to confront it. We also need to admit that it's not ancient history. There is still racism, all the way from the highest levels of government down to those stupid toys. You're strong, and you're wise beyond your years. That's why I knew you could see aspects of life in this country through the lens of your strength and wisdom. Do you still want to continue on to Memphis and New Orleans?"

"Tunde, there is nowhere I would rather be than in the passenger seat of this Jeep, being mentored by you. Lead on!"

Tunde smiled and relaxed at the wheel. The sun was getting low in the west. She was looking forward to introducing Olorin to some real Memphis music, but first, some real Memphis barbecue!

They pulled into the Bluff City right around supper time.

"Our first stop is on Madison Avenue: Berretta's Barbecue. We won't have trouble finding a table because we won't even get out of the car!"

There was no missing Berretta's. A tall neon sign featured a waiter holding aloft a plate of french fries, standing on a huge red arrow pointing into the parking lot. Tunde pulled under an awning that covered half of the paved area. Large overhead signs posted the menu. After they perused the selections, she flashed the Jeep's headlights to signal that they were ready to order. A waiter emerged from the building, looking just like his overhead neon likeness. They gave him their order, and fifteen minutes later he appeared with a tray that clipped on to their open car-window frame. It was piled high: pork ribs with honey-sweetened sauce, cole slaw, and hushpuppies, along with two bottles of Tru Ade orange soda.

"Olorin, I think our twenty-four-hour fast after the half-smoke feast in DC has gone on long enough. Agreed?"

"Agreed!"

They dug in.

After handing off their empty paper plates, soda bottles, and several dozen napkins soaked in sauce to the waiter, Tunde announced their next destination.

"I think it's time we heard some Memphis-style music. Next stop, Beale Street!"

CHAPTER 9

CLUB SATCHMO

On the drive across town, Olorin filled Tunde in on a bit of African culinary lore.

"We have barbecue in Nigeria. We call it *suya*. It's beef, chicken, or fish slow-cooked with garlic, ginger, peanuts, and the main ingredient, hot Scotch bonnet peppers."

"You could open your own place here in Memphis. Olorin's Suya Shop!"

"I think that might cut into my academic studies…"

"Just a little bit, but it might be worth it! Hey, here's the place."

On the corner of Beale and Hernando Streets stood an imposing three-story building. A large sign read:

PANTAGES DRUG STORE

And a smaller sign above it read:

CLUB SATCHMO

Admission was three dollars total for the two travelers to climb the stairs to the second-floor nightclub. They were greeted by a jovial, portly man in a double-breasted sharkskin zoot suit.

"Good evening, ladies. Allow me to introduce myself. My name is Moonbeam Morris. I'm the proprietor of this establishment, and I'm guessing y'all are from out of town. Well, welcome to Club Satchmo, named after the great jazz musician Louis Armstrong. Down in the Big Easy, we used to call him Satchel Mouth!"

Moonbeam gave a hearty laugh.

"Here at Club Satchmo, we feature the finest artists in blues, jazz, and rhythm and blues. Tonight, you are in for a treat when C.C. Lloyd takes the stage!"

He gestured broadly toward the stage, flashing a gold tooth. Then he sat down at their table, adjusting his silk necktie.

"I bet you young folks are Elvis Presley fans. He's quite the singer and dancer, isn't he? Do you know where he learned how to sing and dance? I'll tell you where. Right here, on our stage! He was here all the time, studying, you might say. Ten years ago, segregation was the law, but I looked the other way when a youngster showed an interest in this music. It's an art form, you know."

He chuckled.

"Sometimes one of the greats would even let Elvis sit in with the band and sing a song. You know, plunge him right into the deep end!"

Moonbeam raised an eyebrow and looked around furtively, as if letting them in on a secret.

"He was a smart boy. He didn't even mind being booed once in a while. He was schoolin' himself. He learned from the best, right here at Club Satchmo."

Moonbeam straightened up and smiled broadly.

"I hope that after the show is over, you ladies will avail yourselves of some fine lodging at the Morris Hotel. It's not far; in fact, all you have to do is walk upstairs, and you'll be in the lobby! My wife, Evangeline, will take good care of you. Now, I must get to work."

The house lights went down, except for a single spotlight shining on Moonbeam.

"Ladies and gentlemen, it's star time! Please give a warm Club Satchmo welcome to the one, the only, Mr. C.C. Lloyd!"

On cue, the stage lights came up and the band launched into an urgent, shuffling beat. Couples left their seats and filled the dance floor. C.C. Lloyd, in a sparkling blue tuxedo jacket, walked onstage, already playing his cherry-red guitar. The notes that he played were like bee stings, sharp and abrupt. He stepped up to the microphone.

"Well, I woke up with the blues, and I've still got 'em now."

Shouts of approval exploded from the audience like fireworks.

"Yes, I woke up with the blues, and baby, I've still got 'em now."

More shouts, egging him on, with a few *amens* sprinkled in.

"They say these blues get better; I sure wish somebody'd show me how."

He punctuated the lines that he sang with plangent notes on the guitar, sometimes stinging but oftentimes wailing and keening. Olorin realized that he was using the guitar like an African talking drum. On a song like "Woke Up with the Blues," he would sing, as if addressing a loved one, and then "she" would answer him, in a voice that might accuse and scold, or soothe and console. It was a continual duet between C.C. and Lola, as he introduced his guitar to the audience. Like the talking drum, which could be squeezed by a skillful player to speak. Lola's strings were squeezed to talk and sing in a call-and-response dialogue with her man.

After C.C. had played several encores and left the stage to a standing ovation, the women thanked Moonbeam and made their way upstairs to rest up for the next day's journey.

CHAPTER 10

THE CROSSROADS

Wednesday, June 21, 1967
Memphis, Tennessee, to Cleveland, Mississippi

In the morning, Tunde and Olorin traveled three blocks west on Beale Street, toward the river, and made a left on South Main. In five minutes, they were at the intersection with Calhoun Street. The building on the corner had a green and red neon sign reading:

THE ARCADE RESTAURANT

They ordered sweet potato pancakes with a side of grits at the oldest surviving eatery in Memphis. After coffee, they parked downtown and strolled the shops along Union Avenue, passing Sun Studio at 706 Union, where rhythm and blues greats recorded in the early 1950s and erstwhile music student Elvis Presley made his own first recordings. As the shadows started leaning to the east, Tunde and Olorin returned to the Jeep. They navigated back to South Main Street and turned left. Twenty minutes later, they crossed the Mississippi border on Highway 61.

The city fell away, replaced by a sea of cotton fields on both sides of the two-lane highway. The cotton was in early bloom, with white and purple blossoms that would be replaced by puffy white bolls in early fall. Both women rode silently for a while. The rural environment looked unchanged since the 1930s, except for the occasional modern car that passed by heading northbound. Olorin spoke first.

"Tunde, this is the summer solstice, the longest twilight of the year. It's almost the full moon. That's tomorrow night, but it will look full tonight. It's a bit eerie to be driving down this lonely stretch of road, don't you think?"

"It's certainly a change after the music and neon lights in Memphis. It seems like we're the only car driving south on this road tonight."

As the shadows lengthened, they continued south on Highway 61. Olorin consulted the Rand McNally atlas.

"It looks like there aren't any sizable towns until we get down around Clarksdale. Another road, Highway 49 coming down from Helena, Arkansas, is going to join up with us pretty soon. Maybe traffic will pick up a bit then."

As they approached the intersection with Highway 49, they were surprised to see a man standing on the gravel shoulder, his thumb pointed south. In that lonely spot, with the sun going down and nothing in sight but the cotton fields extending to the horizons, Tunde pulled the Jeep over.

"Good evening, sir. Do you need a lift?"

"Oh yes, ma'am. The day is nearly over, and I don't want to be caught out here after sundown, especially with the strawberry moon so bright."

"We'll make room for you. How far are you going?"

"Just to Dockery. Do you know Joe Rice Dockery's place?"

"We're not from around here."

"Neither am I."

The stranger settled in the back seat.

"Dockery's farm is on State Road 8, down on the Little Sunflower River. You just keep goin' south on 49, then turn west at Ruleville, toward Cleveland. You'll go right through the farm. Drop me off there, and you can roll on into Cleveland, or keep going all the way to Rosedale, on the riverside."

"Well, I'm Ayotunde, and this is Olorin."

"They call me Esu."

Olorin, in a sudden involuntary reflex, jerked forward, then took a deep breath and sat back in the passenger seat, her senses heightened.

"Where are you ladies from, if I might ask?"

"I'm from New York State."

Olorin hesitated.

"I'm...I'm from New York State as well."

Tunde shot her a glance. Olorin shook her head ever so slightly, so Tunde let the omission stand.

They passed a sign that read:

ENTERING SUNFLOWER COUNTY

They continued south, in the silence that settles over fellow travelers as the sky outside turns dark. The Jeep's headlights illuminated another sign.

PARCHMAN STATE PENITENTIARY

Tunde glanced over at Olorin. Her eyes were closed. She was chanting very softly under her breath.

"Esu ljelu, esu ljelu."

Esu leaned forward from the back seat. Olorin bit her lip and stopped chanting.

"Ma'am, would you mind speeding up for the next few miles? This is a bad stretch of road."

Olorin kept her eyes on the two-lane road as Tunde answered. "I saw the word *penitentiary*, but I don't see a big building or a wall, like Sing Sing, up where we live."

"This place is different from Sing Sing. It's a farm. No, I'll tell you like it is. It's a plantation. Just like before 1865. Can I tell you something that most Northerners like yourselves don't know?"

"Of course, Esu."

Olorin shuddered again at the mention of his name.

"You've heard of the Thirteenth Amendment, the one that outlawed slavery."

"We were just talking about it the other day. Juneteenth."

Tunde slowed down while a possum crossed the road, his yellow eyes glaring in the headlight beams.

"Well, ladies, Juneteenth or no Juneteenth, the wording says that slavery is outlawed unless a person is convicted of a crime. It doesn't say what kind of crime. So you see, the state is free to round up able-bodied men to work the fields without pay, without freedom. They just have to be convicted of some crime."

Esu paused and took a couple of labored deep breaths.

"Are some of 'em real violent criminals? No doubt about that, ladies. It's rough in there, I can tell you. But there are three thousand men sleeping in bunkhouses out in those fields. They're roused before dawn at gunpoint and chop cotton until sunset. If they try to leave, they're tracked down by dogs. In other words, they're slaves. We're passing through a slave plantation right now. That's why I asked you to speed up. This is an unholy place."

The sun disappeared in a blaze of red clouds to the west, and the strawberry moon, looking just like a full moon, rose in the east. Esu grew edgy.

"Ruleville is just up ahead. Turn right on Highway 8. You can open it up then. It's only five miles."

He was shifting uncomfortably in the back seat as she made the turn.

"Step on it, please. We're almost there. You'll see the chapel on the right."

"Is Dockery a cotton business?"

"Cotton, lumber. It's mostly known around Sunflower County for music. The front porch of the company store is where Charley Patton, Robert Johnson, and Howlin' Wolf used to sing for the workers. Then they'd all cross the rickety footbridge over the Little Sunflower to the frolic house and barrelhouse all night long."

His breathing picked up.

"You can slow down now. It's on the right. There's the chapel. The store is just beyond it, and there's the footbridge. Let me out now. I got to get across that bridge!"

The moonlight was almost like daylight pouring down on the chapel and the massive cotton gin as Esu ran full tilt toward the bridge, disappearing into the darkness.

Tunde pulled in front of the commissary and backed up, being careful to avoid a large round water trough. As she pulled forward to rejoin Highway 8, the two women clearly heard a wolf howl in the white oak trees across the river.

They continued onward to Cleveland, where they found friendly lodging at a guesthouse listed in the *Traveler's Green Book*. In the morning they would continue south.

CHAPTER 11

INTO THE UNKNOWN

Thursday, June 22, 1967
Cleveland, Mississippi, to New Orleans

Driving down Highway 61 in broad daylight, Tunde felt a little silly about her unease the night before, driving the stranger through those dark, desolate cotton fields in the moonlight. Olorin broke the meditative silence.

"Tunde, do you know why I didn't tell the hitchhiker that I am Yoruba?"

"No, I don't. I was confused by that, and by your whispering, but I didn't want to ask."

"Tunde, that was a visitation. Esu is the Yorba, the trickster god of crossroads. I was whispering a chant of protection. He's unpredictable. Encountering him means we've left the familiar behind and we're heading into the unknown."

Near Vicksburg, they stopped for gas. The attendant took a long look at their car, from front to back.

"One of them new Jeep Wagoneers. That's a pretty fancy vehicle for a couple of…"

He chewed reflectively on his tobacco for a moment, choosing his next word.

"Ladies. A couple of ladies."

He spit his tobacco.

"Where y'all hail from?"

"I'm from New York."

"New York."

He snorted.

"Heard a lot about what goes on up there."

"And I'm from Nigeria."

"Well, I'll be! Nigeria. Ain't that in Africa?"

"Yes, that's indeed where it is."

He examined Olorin's face quizzically.

"And you speak English?"

Olorin smiled and assumed her most posh queen's English.

"One would hope so, considering that English is our official language, although to avoid obfuscation in a capacious former British colony with a multitude of autochthonous tongues still extant, it's efficacious to sharpen one's rhetorical acumen by becoming a bit of a linguist."

She smiled again at the puzzled attendant and dropped the posh accent.

"And now, please fill 'er up!"

Tank filled, they continued south toward New Orleans.

CHAPTER 12

THE BIG EASY

Thursday, June 22, 1967
New Orleans, Louisiana

Ayotunde and Olorin checked into the Cornstalk Fence Hotel on Royal Street in the French Quarter. Their room occupied the second floor of a Louis XV–inspired tower with crenelated battlements. It was decorated in the old French plantation style, with a pair of four-poster beds, a fireplace, a stained-glass bay window in the alcove formed by the round tower, and a balcony where guests could read or simply watch the goings-on below in the heart of the Vieux Carre. Of course, the courtyard facing Royal Street was bordered by a wrought-iron fence cast in the form of a row of cornstalks. The two women dropped their suitcases in their room, stashed the Jeep in a parking spot, and took off on an urban hike around the Quarter.

Turning right on Royal, they crossed Dumaine and took the next right on Saint Ann Street, crossing old thoroughfares that recalled times and places in the French history of the Crescent

City: Bourbon Street, Dauphine Street, Burgundy Street. They strolled through a district of pastel cottages with hurricane shutters framing the windows. There was a coffeehouse or a tavern on every corner, with small art galleries and shops scattered in between.

Half a block short of Rampart Street, they stopped at 1020 Saint Ann Street, the former site of Marie Catherine Laveau's house in the 1800s. Marie Catherine was characterized in latter days as the voodoo queen of New Orleans, but in her own time she was a priestess and healer who sat with the sick and the imprisoned, fought against the death penalty, and administered advice and herbal remedies to the upper crust of the city. She was also a hairdresser to the well-heeled matrons, and by keeping her ears open she gathered an ever-flowing stream of gossip, rumor, and closely held secrets that aided in her consultations and created a mystique enhanced by rumors that she certainly must be psychic.

"Voodoo. Back in those days, Olorin, if a woman in a European colony practiced the healing arts that are an everyday part of life where you grew up, it was whispered that she was a voodoo queen, maybe even a witch. In New England she would have been put on trial and tortured, but the French were laissez-faire about such things. In fact, Madame Laveau was one of the pillars of New Orleans society."

"Tunde, you're talking about the 1800s. Wasn't she a slave?"

"Marie Catherine was a free Creole. She was a mix of African, French, and Native American blood, a beautiful mélange of cultures. She married a Haitian Creole man named Jacques Paris, and I'm sure that French was her first language, but there was still a strong presence of Yoruba wisdom in Louisiana back then."

Both women yawned. They were feeling the fatigue of the five-day trek down from New York, so with just enough energy to hike back to the hotel, they turned in early.

CHAPTER 13

THE CARRIAGE DRIVER

Friday, June 23, 1967
New Orleans, Louisiana

In the morning, they sat out on their balcony, looking down on the awakening city while they adjusted to the dense Gulf Coast humidity.

"Tunde, I'm sensing something in the air here in New Orleans. Maybe it's the scent of spices that remind me of home in Nigeria. It makes me feel like there's still Yoruba magic here."

"I have that feeling, too, but it's not something you can look for. Maybe it finds you. Hey, speaking of spices, I'm getting a little bit hungry. Let's find an outdoor café and grab a light breakfast."

Over cups of strong coffee with chicory and a shared plate of beignets, sweet morsels of *choux* pastry, deep-fried and rolled in cane sugar, they discussed plans for their visit to the Crescent City. While they conspired, a brass band paraded by the open-air Café du Monde *terrasse*.

"I was hoping to hear music, Tunde, maybe some blues and jazz. I figured that would mean going to a nightclub, but now I get the feeling that there's music in the air all the time here!"

"Olorin, I get a feeling that jazz, blues, and gospel sprang like a fountain right from this very neighborhood, and then it flowed all over the world."

"Remember when Moonbeam called Louis Armstrong Satchmo? The old folks in Nigeria still talk about the day that he came to our country. When the airplane door opened, it's said that he stood at the top of the gangway and blew his trumpet, while hundreds of my ancestors danced joyfully on the tarmac. Music really is a universal language, isn't it?"

"One thing that interests me is the celebration tomorrow, June twenty-fourth. It's the feast of Jean Baptiste. That dates all the way back to French rule when Louis XV was the monarch and ruler of New Orleans. It's a bit strange to think that where we are sitting right now, after driving down from Westchester, was part of France for many years. I'm interested to see what goes on tomorrow on the feast day."

They paid their tab, left a tip on their *en plein air* table, and walked toward Decatur Street. Just as they reached the curb, a carriage pulled up, pulled by a beautiful palomino and driven by a man in red velvet eighteenth-century French chevalier garb. He bowed, tipping his plumed tricorne hat.

"Hop in, ladies! There is much to see and do, and time will not stand still for us!"

Tunde smiled at Olorin and shrugged. They clambered up into the carriage.

The big wooden wheels clattered over cobblestones.

"Allow me to introduce myself, *jeunes filles*. My name today is Sam. Sam Riparian *a votre service*!"

Tunde laughed.

"Is that name really only for today, Sam?"

"Oh yes! One must not get stuck on one name for too long."

"But what did your parents name you?"

"My parents? Oh, that's a tough one, *jeune fille*. That was a very long time ago. I was called Shem-el in the distant past, but there have been many names since then. Nowadays I prefer just Sam Riparian. Man of the river."

"Okay then. Sam it is. My name is Ayotunde, but everyone calls me Tunde. This is Olorin."

"Ah, you are joy, and she is an artist. How lovely! It's a pleasure to have you aboard."

Tunde was a bit surprised that their carriage driver instantly knew the Yoruba meaning of their African names. Olorin's forehead crinkled thoughtfully. Tunde glanced around quizzically.

"Could I ask where we're going, Sam?"

"Oh gosh, I haven't really thought about that. Where would you like to go?"

Tunde and Olorin exchanged glances, smiling. He was certainly eccentric.

"Well, to see the sights, I suppose."

"The sights! Well, there are a lot of sights. Here's one right now. Whoa, Bucephalus!"

The palomino came to an obedient halt.

"We were here yesterday, Sam. Where Marie Catherine Laveau's house was."

"You were indeed here yesterday."

The two women exchanged glances again, puzzled this time.

"She was a great woman. We all knew her as Catherine. Did you know that many French girls back in those days were named Marie at birth, after the Blessed Virgin? They used their middle names as they grew up and bore their own children, who they also named Marie, or Joseph if they were boys."

"And I suppose you also knew the Blessed Virgin and Saint Joseph?"

Sam simply made a *chuck* sound and snapped the reins to get the palomino trotting again.

The carriage halted at the end of the block, where Saint Ann Street came to a *T*.

"Across the street, my ladies, is Congo Square. That was the gathering place for folks of African descent. Slaves, freed slaves, and Creoles could celebrate, create music, and make magic. It was a place for the community to dance the *bamboula* and the *juba*."

He paused, reflecting.

"Oh, that was a time. Such a time. It was a moment of freedom. You can still hear that in the music today, the music that started here. That's why people all over the world love it."

"I'll bet you were a real Casanova back then, Sam."

"Oh, you mean with the ladies?"

He chuckled.

"I had my fun, all right. In fact, I sat next to Giacomo, the real Casanova, at the premiere of *Don Giovanni*. Yes, Prague was something back in those days; the ladies fluttering like butterflies at the opera house, dressed in their *crinolettes*. And Mozart; he was quite a character. Oh yes, he was, but to tell you more would break a gentlemen's code."

He snapped the reins.

"Now, this is Rampart Street. We'd be at the north end of town now, back in 1798 or thereabouts. This was the ramparts, the city walls. Beyond this there was nothing but cypress swamp and snakes all the way to the *grande* lake, except for the *ville des morts*. We're coming to it now. Old Number One. Behind that wall, Marie Catherine rests from her labors."

"It's a bit spooky, isn't it?"

"The old ones tell us that the best teachers are the dead. I've learned a lot from the residents of that city there."

The palomino, without being prompted, trotted onward for a short way.

"Looking north for a few blocks on Basin Street is where Storyville used to be. There was some revelry going on there, I tell you, and music playing around the clock. They say that's where jazz was born. Kid Ory, King Oliver, Buddy Bolden, Jelly Roll Morton…"

He paused, with his eyes closed.

"Oh, didn't we ramble back then! Now, you ladies must be getting hungry."

"I knew you were psychic, Sam!"

"Don't even think about the tourist restaurants. I will give you a taste of the real thing."

He clucked to bring the palomino to a rapid canter.

Sam shouted back to the women, over the tattoo of horseshoes drumming on cobblestones.

"We're traveling along the Bayou Saint John. This was the old route through the swamp to the lake. The city begins to fade out here, where the fog sweeps in off the black water."

As if on cue, they did indeed roll into a thick bank of fog. Sam began singing a song.

"The rain, it raineth every day on kings and queens, clowns and carriage drivers alike!"

He roared with laughter, snapped the reins, and shouted, "Faster Bucephalus. Faster!"

The palomino broke into a gallop and raced through the thick fog. Tunde and Olorin got the sense that wherever the carriage was racing to, it wasn't a normal restaurant. Had they felt any trepidation, they might well have leapt from the carriage, risking a few bruises rather than galloping headlong into a foggy swamp, but there was something about Sam that intrigued them both. How did he know certain things about them already, and why did he make comments that suggested he had been around for centuries? In any case, he was elderly, like a jolly eccentric grandpa. There simply was nothing threatening about him, but there was much that piqued their curiosity. While Sam kept his eyes on the road, Tunde lowered her head just a little bit and gave Olorin a shrug and a raised-eyebrow look that said, *We came down here for adventure, didn't we?* Olorin returned the look with a nod that said, *Remember, Tunde, we've entered the unknown.*

They settled back in the carriage seat, wondering what might happen next.

CHAPTER 14

THE CABIN

The carriage came to a stop on a dry hillock, what swamp people call an island. Sam tied up his horse and helped Tunde and Olorin dismount from the carriage. A dilapidated cabin stood under a canopy of live oaks draped with Spanish moss. The building looked as if it had grown there, like the trees around it.

"I do hope the ride wasn't too rough! Please let yourselves into the cabin and make yourselves at home."

He patted the palomino on the flank and spoke to her in a soft tone.

"Good girl. Now let's get you dried off and put away for a little while."

Tunde reached out and patted the horse gently. The big animal shook her mane and gave an appreciative snort.

"Your horse is beautiful. What's her name again?"

"Bucephalus. Yes, that's it. Bucephalus."

He patted the horse again.

"Good girl."

Without turning away from the horse, he said softly.

"Alexander gave her that name, when he was a little boy."

"Did Alexander grow up around here?"

The old man shook his head reflectively.

"Oh, no. He was someone I knew a very long time ago. Now run inside. I'll be along shortly."

Sam stabled the palomino. Then he sighed, clomped up the rickety steps, pushed open the weathered screen door, and tied a Tabasco sauce–stained apron around his waist.

"I believe you young people wanted to sample some real Louisiana *lagniappe*?"

He bowed and made a comical sweeping gesture.

"You have come to the right place. Welcome to Back-swamp Manor!"

Sam roared again with laughter.

"Now, help me drain these shrimp through the strainer so we can let them cool while we prepare our roux!"

He rolled up the puffy linen sleeves of his carriage livery blouse and stepped into the role of chef de cuisine.

"Tunde, leave the flame burning, and put that cast iron skillet on to heat up. Olorin, grease the pan with fatback. Now dice an onion and slice up those peppers. Sauté 'em in that nice fat. *Magnifique*! Here we go now. Toss in the sausage and brown it up good. Finish it off with the sliced okra. Tunde, check on those shrimp! There's a jar on the shelf with bay leaves. Grab a couple of those for later. We'll toss 'em in and fish 'em out, just like a couple of perch."

While they worked, Sam broke into his song again.

"The rain, it raineth every day, on kings and queens, clowns and carriage drivers alike."

More bacon fat was whisked with flour in a big wooden bowl, and then sassafras filé was tossed in. The sausage came out of the skillet and the roux mix went in.

"I learned this from the Choctaw. When the roux is thick and brown, we put everything together in the skillet. Let's heat up some rice."

Sausage, shrimp, peppers, onions, and okra went in, with a splash of Tabasco sauce. The cabin was infused with a perfume that cast a beatific spell. While the cooking warmth permeated the room, Sam sat down, lit his pipe, and smiled, Buddha-like. He sang a ditty.

"I was born about ten thousand years ago, and there's nothing in this world that I don't know. I saw Peter, Paul, and Moses playing ring around the roses, and I'll lick the man who says it isn't so!"

Sam laughed and put his pipe in a tin cup.

"Let's eat!"

After they downed heaping platefuls of rice and seafood smothered in the brown roux étouffée, Sam went out to the icehouse and dragged in a cooler. He spooned crusty apple pandowdy, sweetened with molasses, onto each plate, and they washed it down with bottles of Big Shot soda pop.

He settled into his easy chair, reached underneath, and pulled out a stoneware jug decorated with a bearded face painted in indigo.

"I'll bet y'all ain't never seen a greybeard jug. This one's from Shrewsbury. Legend has it that Henry Tudor quaffed from this very vessel."

Sam took a long draft from the jug, recorked it, and wiped his lips.

"Now, ladies. If everyone has a comfortable chair, I suggest we all get a nap. We have business on the Bayou Saint John at midnight, the first moment of the feast of Jean Baptiste."

"What happens then?"

"Well, several things. To start, we pick the first summer blooms of pennyjohn. That must be done only by moonlight. Then we collect fennel to hang on doors for protection against the jumbie, and we pick foxfire for charms. A strong medicine woman can cast a spell with that stuff, make somebody's limbs go limp.

"Tomorrow in the daylight the lodges will be on parade, the Masons and the Templars. The Zulu Social Aid and Pleasure Club will lead the second line, and the Wild Tchoupitoulas will do their war dance. Bones will be burned in the festal fire, so ashes can be spread on the crops. It's all preordained. Your presence is preordained, too. Why do you think I summoned you here, all the way from New York?"

"You summoned us?"

"I did. Tonight, on the bayou, we will need your help."

"What kind of help?"

"Help recovering the stolen trick bag."

"Trick bag? Before you tell us what that is, how long ago was it stolen?"

"Oh! It hasn't happened yet."

"How can we help you recover something that hasn't been stolen yet?"

"Don't worry too much about the ordering of time. It will happen tonight, and then your mission will begin."

"Our mission?"

"Your mission. Y'all are sleuths, gumshoes, detectives, aren't you?"

"Well, sort of, but how did you know?"

"*Cherie*, do you think I've stayed out of Parchman this long without knowing how to recognize the law when I see it?"

Sam laughed at the thought, and his eyes started growing heavy. He nodded, and his chin fell on his chest.

Tunde and Olorin were silent, but they met each other's eyes in a signal of mutual wonder. Neither woman was sleepy. They were stranded in a swamp cabin with a man who moved in and out of a fortune-telling trance, a man who claimed to have summoned them to the dark bayou. It was too much to absorb and even think about sleeping. While they sat in silence, the logs in the woodstove turned to glowing bars.

Suddenly, Sam stopped snoring and raised his head.

His eyes were gazing straight ahead. There was no evidence that he was aware of the two women in his one-room cabin. He began to speak, murmuring in short phrases, like patches and rags of cloth.

"My home…my home is in the summer stars.

"I was on the galaxy at creation.

"I spoke before there was speech.

"I have drifted like the river. I have been many things."

He paused. A limpkin cried out in the swamp.

"I shall be on earth 'til the day of doom, and it is not known whether I am fish or flesh."

His chin fell to his chest again.

The girls sat in silence while the last embers glowed. Sam spoke again.

"I have fled as fog, and as a wolf howling in the wilderness. I was Loup-Garou, and Wendigo, and I was Kitsune, the nine-tailed fox."

He took a long, laborious breath.

"I was laid down for three days on a rattlesnake skin, then set adrift in a leather bag until I washed up on the shore of the grande lake."

His chin fell again. After a short pause, he raised his head, opened his eyes, and stared directly at the two women.

"You should know that there is another dreamer, dreaming us."

His chin went down once more, and once again he began snoring.

The two women suddenly felt overcome by waves of sleep, and as the embers went dark, the cabin on the swamp was quiet.

CHAPTER 15

THE TRICK BAG

The tin coffee pot banged loudly down onto the woodstove.

"Rise and shine! Ten p.m.! Time to prepare for the eve of Jean Baptiste!"

Tunde and Olorin rubbed their eyes and looked around, feeling strangely refreshed after just two hours of sleep. The comforting smell of percolating coffee filled the cabin.

"Let me tell you a few things now, because we won't be able to converse at the ceremony. Sister Malvina Latour will be presiding. She usually resides across the lake, deep in the Honey Island swamp, but every year on the twenty-third of June at sundown, she paddles slowly across to the bank of the Bayou Saint John to make a nation sack, a trick bag to conjure with. Tonight at midnight she'll be using flowers and ginseng roots. Those'll be mixed with limewash powder and salt scraped from the plaster of Marie Catherine's tomb, and it will all be shaken in a red flannel bag. Once the nation sack is closed and Malvina utters her spell, it must never be opened again."

He poured three cups of strong coffee.

"Tonight, there will be treachery. Marie Pompadour, who claims to be the ghost of King Louis's consort, will paddle in a pirogue from her lair under the old Indian mound at Star Bayou, far beyond Rigolet's Pass and Alligator Bend. While Sister Malvina is in her trance, the witch Madame Pompadour will leap up from the bayou and steal the conjure bag. She must not be allowed to escape. The bag is an amulet for protection, but it can be turned around and become a talisman for power, power that can be used for black magic."

Sam drained the last of his coffee mug.

"We, the followers of Marie Catherine Laveau, do not practice black magic. We are healers and advisers. We can't let the nation sack fall into the hands of that witch. She's been building her power under the Indian mound for two hundred years. She could cast a spell over the entire city."

"What can we do to help, Sam?"

"I'll be doing what I can, Olorin. I trace my bloodline back to Sobek the crocodile god on the Nile. If Pompadour tries to escape on the bayou, I will use my power to stop her, but that may not be enough."

He turned to Ayotunde.

"You have a car. At the Cornstalk Fence Hotel?"

She had learned not to ask how he knew such things.

"Yes, a Jeep with four-wheel drive."

"Bucephalus will take us there in an instant. You recall Congo Square, of course?"

"Of course."

"After you descend from the carriage at the hotel, Bucephalus and I will continue on to the fete. You two will need your car to get to the fete. I may not be around at the end. We will all meet again at the site, on the bank of the Bayou Saint John. To get there, drive north on Saint Ann Street and turn right on Rampart Street, at the square. Drive into the Seventh Ward and turn left on Saint Bernard Avenue. That will take you all the way through Faubourg Tremé to the Bayou Saint John. You will park your car on the bridge to Demourelles Island. I will be waiting for you. As we pass through the woods, we will pick pennyjohn blossoms and the glowing foxfire for the ceremony. Sister Malvina will be the presiding *mambo* at the ceremony. Others will be there, dancing and shouting the *juré*, pounding the *clave* rhythm on salt-meat kegs. They'll make a sign on the ground out of corn-meal and ashes to invoke John Henry, the steel-driving man. He is two brothers in one man. John is Shango, the god of thunder, and Henry is Ogun, who wields iron. The sign will invest the *gris gris* with power. Once Sister Malvina has sealed the *juju* bag, she will stand on a stone stairway by the waterside on the shore of the bayou. She will enter into her trance while the rest of us moan low, eyes closed. That's when the treachery will occur. It will come to pass. I have already seen it. When Sister Malvina concludes murmuring the words of the spell of power, Madame Pompadour will manifest out of the darkness. She will snatch the conjure bag and then paddle at great speed in her pirogue toward the lake. If she reaches the big water, there will be no way to retrieve the bag, and all will be lost."

Sam paused and caught his breath.

"Remember what I say. There will be no chance for me to repeat it. When Madame Pompadour tries to escape, I will pursue on water. Olorin, you will be mounted on Bucephalus. Both of you will cross the Harrison Avenue Bridge to the west bank of the bayou. Tunde, you will turn north on Wisner Boulevard. The bayou will be on your right, all the way to the lake. Olorin, you will be riding Bucephalus north on the Wisner trail, on the bank of the bayou. The moon will be your only light. You will pass the

Mirabeau Avenue Bridge, the Fillmore Avenue Bridge, and the Lee Bridge. Keep going, and don't slow down. When you reach the Lakeshore Drive bridge, wait there. You will see Pompadour racing in her pirogue, with me in pursuit, but if I'm unable to overtake her, or if I haven't survived the chase, it will be up to you two to stop her. You must not let her cross under the bridge and reach the lake. One more thing. Just short of the last bridge, you will see the floodgate. It's a steel and concrete structure, thirty feet tall and sixty feet wide across the bayou. That will not stop her, and it will not stop me, either."

Sam hitched the carriage and the two women climbed aboard. Sam, in his red velvet waistcoat and plumed hat, snapped the reins.

"*Alons,* Bucephalus, *galop*!

CHAPTER 16

THE FETE

The trio reconvened at the Demourelles Island Bridge. They crossed on foot and entered a dense bank of fog that enclosed the small island like a castle wall. They followed Sam along the old Choctaw footpath, picking fennel, pennyjohn, and luminous foxfire as they made their way through dense thickets of sugarberry and turtle grass, swatting at lariats of Spanish moss that hung from the cypress and live oak trees. As they neared the mainstream of the bayou, lantern light glowed like a firefly in the fog.

Sister Malvina was standing on the stone steps, facing the water. She was tall, with great hoops hanging from her ears. Her head was swathed in a red flannel *tignon*, a headscarf worn in the 1800s by decree of the *maire de New Orleans*, who considered the hairstyles of African women an occasion of sin, offering too much carnal temptation to the white men of the city. Of course, the women of the Crescent City embraced the law with enthusiasm, creating elaborate, glamourous *tignons* that served only to enhance their allure.

Sister Malvina wore an ankle length blue gown, with a red shawl that wrapped around her shoulders. As she filled the flannel bag with flowers and roots, a lizard's tail, and a handful of graveyard dust from Old Number One, she chanted softly. Once the bag was filled to her satisfaction, she tied it with a leather thong. The lantern was extinguished. Sister Malvina closed her eyes. She began reciting the prayer that would invest the bag with power.

"Egun, Ifa, Ibea…"

To Tunde's surprise, Olorin joined in, whispering.

"Ire, Osun…"

As the name of the Yoruba river goddess was intoned, a woman in the elaborate French dress and hairstyle of eighteenth-century Versailles leapt from the bayou onto the stone stairs and in a single motion grabbed the juju bag and disappeared into the darkness. Sam shouted.

"*Alons!* Don't let her escape!"

He threw down his coat and plumed hat and dove into the black water.

Tunde and Olorin raced through the cypress grove and crossed the bridge. As Tunde turned the ignition key, Olorin was already astride Bucephalus, galloping toward the Harrison Avenue Bridge. On the west bank of the bayou, they turned north: Tunde on Wisner Boulevard and Olorin on the palomino in full gallop on Wisner Trail, down by the waterside.

The pirogue was moving up the center of the bayou at the speed of a powerboat, not like any ordinary dugout canoe. Behind her was another entity, also quite out of the ordinary. Two glowing eyes projected above the surface, trailed by a foaming wake. When it broke the surface momentarily, Olorin saw it clearly. A twelve-foot alligator, moving at a speed to nearly match the demonic pirogue, was in pursuit of the witch.

They passed the Mirabeau Avenue Bridge, the Fillmore Avenue Bridge, and the Lee Bridge. Ahead, they could see the lights of the concrete floodgate, stretched like a massive dam across the bayou. Olorin brought Bucephalus to a canter, then a trot, and spoke softly. "Whoa, girl. Let's see what happens here."

Horse and woman both stared wide-eyed as the pirogue barreled at full speed toward the gate, then lifted like a seaplane and soared over the thirty-foot structure, landing with a reverberant splash. Their eyes grew even wider as the alligator did the same. Olorin snapped the reins.

"*Alons,* Bucephalus. *Galop!*"

The palomino and the Jeep converged on the Lakeshore Drive Bridge. Madame Pompadour was racing toward them. The power that she drew from her long sleep under the Indian mound was propelling her with superhuman force. In her wake, the alligator was falling behind. It looked like there was no way to prevent her from crossing under the bridge and entering the lake. From there, she would have open water to complete her escape through Rigolet's Pass and then the Gulf of Mexico to the Atlantic Ocean. Ayotunde was on the verge of panic.

"Olorin, what do we do?"

Her young companion didn't answer. Tunde glanced over at her. Olorin was standing very still. She stared, without blinking, down at the witch. She pointed with her left hand and intoned loudly.

"Egun, Ifa, Ibea, Ire, Osun!"

With her right hand she tossed a sprig of glowing foxfire directly into the pirogue as it reached the bridge. She pointed downward and shouted.

"*Mi ni ire*! Osun, goddess of the river, bring us good fortune!"

Madame Pompadour's paddle froze midstroke. She stiffened and stared blankly, zombielike. The pirogue slowed to a crawl and drifted as if it were floating on molasses. It disappeared under the bridge.

The pirogue did not emerge from the other side of the bridge. The alligator bore down at full speed and charged hell-for-leather under the structure. The two women, standing in the dark on the Lakeshore Bridge pavement, heard splashing and a muffled scream. Then the bayou fell silent.

Tunde looked wide-eyed at her crimefighting partner.

"Wow, Olorin. You're the real deal!"

"I learned things growing up back where we first met, by the sacred river of Osun. I was trained by the *Iyalowo*, the priestess. Sculpting the *orishas*, the helpful goddesses, I took on some of their power. That's what we believe to be the power of art, in Yorubaland."

Ayotunde gazed down at the dark bayou where a spell had just been cast.

"Olorin, after tonight, that's my belief, too."

The younger girl suddenly felt exhausted. She turned to mount Bucephalus, but the beautiful palomino had vanished into the night.

In the Jeep, Tunde and Olorin retraced their path south to the Harrison Avenue Bridge. They turned south again on Saint Bernard Avenue and drove slowly through the silent Tremé neighborhood. It was time to get some sleep at the Cornstalk Fence Hotel.

In the morning, they woke up refreshed and began the long trek north, skipping the day-long parades, which seemed like they might be a bit anticlimactic after their breathless midnight chase.

As they crossed Lake Pontchartrain, Tunde glanced over at Olorin, who was wide-eyed in wonder at the vastness of the *grande lac*. Tunde thought back once again to her first mission, at the castle in the west of Ireland, and how she responded instinctively when Artemis was in need of rescue. She had never seen herself as a hero, but she had grown so much in a short time as a protégé secret agent. Now, as she saw Olorin's enthusiasm, and having witnessed the power of her Yoruba magic, she couldn't help but wonder if she and her young traveling companion would indeed be the next crimefighting team. After all, Artemis had been canvassing the globe for years before Tunde even came to Sarah Lawrence. Would there come a time when she would want to relax, and Tunde would be called to step into her shoes?

The two rode in silence across the great lake, reflecting on the events of the last few days, and wondering what further adventure lay ahead.

Three days later they were safely ensconced at the Atalanta estate. They regaled Artemis with tales of their exploits down the back roads of America, and she filled them in on her, as she put it, "everyday" job guarding the art exhibit. Still absorbed in the dark meaning of her two mysterious dreams, she kept that part of her latest beau geste secret.

Late summer in Valhalla finally brought the respite that Artemis had hoped for, but come autumn, that would change.

PART THREE

The Bernini Spear

CHAPTER 17

THE LUNCHEON

Sunday, October 8, 1967
Strabo Headquarters, New York City

Kevin Macduff was greeting a stream of donors arriving in taxis and limos at Strabo headquarters. His job had shifted in his first three years from organizing expeditions and cataloging specimens to coddling the donors who kept the program alive. He accepted the responsibility, and with younger members like Artemis, Ayotunde, and Olorin out in the field, he was content to focus on keeping the bills paid back home. This early autumn luncheon was a warm-up for the annual fundraiser on New Year's Day. After a meal of bison burgers with a side of dandelion salad, coffee was poured, and Macduff walked to the podium.

"Many thanks to one and all for your generous support! With bison on the rebound in the American West, we decided to be ahead of the curve and serve burgers to you now, before they go on sale at Tad's Steakhouse!"

Genial laughter and a few shouts of approval. Kevin continued.

"This year we have experienced the greatest membership growth in the club's history. The advent of affordable jet travel means that globetrotting is no longer the exclusive province of intrepid explorers. Now, even the trepid can scale peaks and plumb oceans!"

More laughter.

"All kidding aside, it's truly an honor to welcome so many new members. For their benefit, I want to offer a very brief history of the club, and if you have heard it all before, I trust you will indulge me for a few minutes.

"The Strabo Society was founded in 1900 by a group of young Yale faculty anthropologists with a taste for adventure. The first director, Duncan Sinclair, was a globetrotting explorer. When he wasn't in far-flung locations, men like Byrd, Amundsen, and Shackleton would spend afternoons consulting with him. From far corners of the world, the Society's members collected artifacts for the Museum of Natural History, and member-published articles were a regular feature of *National Geographic*. The club's high profile attracted New York City's most generous contributors, and by 1940 a new building, this one, was leased here on the Upper East Side. That was the same year that Duncan Sinclair went into semiretirement, keeping a watchful eye on the administration of his successor, Charles Iverson. Mr. Iverson was initiated back in 1920, and during the next two decades he held off bandits while he searched for fossils in the Gobi Desert. He was once ransomed by a certain Yale fraternity after he was kidnapped by smugglers in the Hindu Kush. He became club director on Duncan Sinclair's retirement in 1940, and on his subsequent retirement in 1963, I had the honor of taking over the job. Our six decades of accomplishment notwithstanding, we are still, as ever, dependent on the generosity and good will of our beloved donors. And now, dessert will be served!"

As he worked the room, shaking hands, kissing cheeks, and chatting, Macduff was mentally reciting the speech he *didn't* give. The speech about how during the twenty years that Duncan Sinclair ran the society while Iverson traveled the globe, the two men developed an extracurricular relationship outside of their normal Society roles. Iverson had discovered that taking inventory of artifacts and artworks in the field, for example, high in the Andes Mountains, was an inexact science to say the least. He began carrying two rucksacks. For every potsherd or Stone Age axe head that went into the Strabo bag, another one went into Iverson's private bag. Over a period of forty years, he and Sinclair amassed a huge collection that went into the Strabo vault, and they were the only two members with the key. This made them fabulously wealthy in a sense, but they didn't cash in their chips. Their "dark" collection was collateral for them to become major dealers on the black market of stolen art and antiquities. They traded using the value of their vault, without having to empty out the contents. It didn't hurt that the Society's prestige was such that they were waved through customs at every airport from New York to Katmandu. Strabo meant prestige, and prestige is always welcome.

It was the perfect cover for what grew into a major criminal enterprise. That is, until the winter of 1960, when they made a fatal mistake. On Sinclair's recommendation, they hired Artemis Fletcher to carry out an assassination. She didn't work out. Her involvement eventually brought down the house of cards, resulting in Iverson's prison sentence and his subsequent maniacal obsession with revenge. Duncan Sinclair? At eighty years of age, his long-suffering liver bailed him out. His funeral was on the same day that Iverson's indictment was handed down.

CHAPTER 18

THE RETURN OF THE NEMESIS

Monday, October 9, 1967
Queens, New York

Charles Iverson filled his pipe, studying the face of the man seated across his "desk"—a battered oak workbench that had served long ago as a taxicab dispatcher's base of operations. The radio switchboard had been torn out when the company went belly-up, and the fixtures were auctioned off. The cabs were long gone, and the empty garage, on a grimy side street in Queens, echoed like a cavern, but Iverson had plans to remedy that emptiness.

After the Strabo Society was busted back in December 1963, Charles "Chuck" Iverson was sentenced to three years of white-collar time for antiquities theft. On June 1, 1964, he handed in his tweed suit at the Danbury federal pen in exchange for prison blues. He spent his time on the inside lecturing on the fine points of Renaissance art for the benefit of his fellow inmates. It's likely that the irony of being lectured on the subject by a convicted art thief wasn't lost on his captive audience, but no one complained. They had their own ironies to gloss over.

Iverson did his full three years. He walked out on June 1, 1967, wearing the same suit he had turned in to the old trusty on day one of his sentence. He was a free man. In his mind, that meant he was free to get back into the lucrative business of global art and antiquities theft. He contacted an old colleague from the Strabo days, a Long Island art collector by the name of Hugo Van Elland. Van Elland had more cash than ethics, and Iverson was able to talk him into fronting him the money for a rack, a shack, and a stack. That is to say: a suit, a place to throw down a cot, and a flow of cash. Iverson also talked the old man into backing him on a heist. Van Elland was planning a big job, a global job, the kind of job he wouldn't entrust to a loose cannon like Iverson, but he agreed to let him handle a small but important element: lining up the collateral he would hold as security to get his major black-market backers in Europe interested. He agreed to front Iverson the cash he would need to hire an underling who could handle the smaller heist. On Monday morning, October 9, a manila envelope arrived in the garage mailbox, just in the nick of time. It was stuffed with two grand in cash. Chuck Iverson was back in business.

It had only taken a few questions at a waterfront dive on the Gowanus Canal to locate a prospect willing and able to do the dirty work: a small-time hood known as Jimmy the Blade. Jimmy's specialty was sawing his way out of jail. After his last escape, through a ceiling vent in his cell on Rikers Island, he melded into the rough-and-tumble fraternity of longshoremen, unloading freight under a variety of aliases and doing odd jobs on the side for shady characters. Jimmy the Blade was summoned to the defunct Gotham Taxi headquarters for his job interview.

Iverson lit his pipe, shook out the match, and tossed it on the floor.

"Jimmy, or whatever your name is today…"

"Jimmy's good."

"I understand you're pretty handy with a saw."

"You might say that. It's been useful to me on occasion."

"Well, I have a job that would put your skill to work, if you're interested."

"A job for how much?"

"A grand. Five in advance, five on completion."

"Go on."

"I need a piece of marble sawed off and brought here."

"Sawed off of what?"

"A statue."

"And brought here from where?"

"Italy. Rome."

"Okay. What's the diameter?"

"About the same as the bars at Rykers."

Jimmy snorted.

"We're talkin' marble, right?"

"That's correct. Marble. Quarried in Siena."

Jimmy the Blade was thoughtful.

"Marble. I would need a steel-frame handsaw, diamond wire blade. Am I supposed to take that over to Italy in my duffel bag?"

"You'll be given an address where you'll be provided with whatever tools you need."

"Okay, where in Rome is this thing?"

"It's in a church, the Santa Maria della Vittoria."

"Stealing from the church? We used to do that when I was a kid in Brooklyn. If you're an altar boy, you've got access."

Iverson tamped his pipe.

"Jimmy, have you ever heard of Gian Lorenzo Bernini?"

"Johnny Bernini? Sure! Arthur Avenue. He was a low-level foot soldier. Storefront arson, that kind of thing. I thought he was still upstate."

Iverson sighed.

"Different Bernini. This one was an Italian sculptor in the late Renaissance. He did a lot of work on the Vatican."

"The Vatican! That's the big time. You thinkin' about hittin' the Vatican?"

It occurred to Iverson that Jimmy, while a numbskull, wasn't totally off base there. A major heist just a few miles from the world's greatest art repository was just the kind of bold statement he needed to make, so soon after getting out of stir. Lost in the anticipation of it all, he found himself weary of engaging Jimmy the Blade in conversation.

"No, we're not hitting the Vatican. Enough talk. Your airline ticket, train ticket, room reservation, and exact instructions are in this envelope. The first five hundred in cash is there as well. The passport has your picture and the name James Fleming. I'll be expecting you back here with the piece on October sixteenth. One week. Got it?

"Got it."

"And don't screw up."

As the garage door slammed down, Iverson settled back in his rickety office chair and poured a glass of Scotch. He raised it in a toast to the empty taxi barn and spoke as if addressing a distinguished audience.

"Here's to sending a message loud and clear to the art world that Chuck Iverson is back in business!"

He reached for his Bic pen and fumbled for a scrap of paper. It was time to drop a teaser in the mail.

CHAPTER 19

THE DAYS THAT NEVER WERE

Wednesday, October 11, 1967
Valhalla, New York

Westchester County at the peak of fall foliage was a picture-perfect scene straight out of a Currier and Ives print. Ayotunde was at the big kitchen window, looking out at the blazing red sugar maples bordering the Atalanta estate, when the phone rang.

"Tunde, this is Kevin Macduff. Is Artemis around?"

"She's in her office."

She covered the receiver with her right palm.

"Fletch, Kevin's on the phone!"

Artemis bounded up the stairs from her basement office, brushing pencil shavings from her flannel shirt.

"Kevin, what's up?"

"Artemis, I know you're busy…"

"Oh yes, indeed, sharpening pencils is hard work. Seriously though, I'm on sabbatical to finish the book I started in France.

I'm twenty thousand words into *From Revolt to Resistance: The Traboules of Lyon.*"

"Okay, you got me. What's a *traboule*?"

"You know, the alleyways, in France! I was tailed there by one of Iverson's stooges back when he was trying to bump me off."

Kevin cleared his throat.

"Artemis, since you bring up Iverson, that's why I called."

She sat down on a kitchen stool.

"Go on."

"A letter came across my desk this morning. No signature or return address. It was short, but not so sweet. I figured you would want to know about right away."

Artemis took a deep breath, to center herself.

"What did it say? Read it to me verbatim."

"Okay. Here goes."

He paused to clear the air.

"You stole the sacred spear from my hands. I can steal sacred spears, too. Beware at the first moment of the day after the days that never were."

Artemis tapped her pencil lightly on her knee, gathering her thoughts.

"Kevin, is Iverson still in prison?"

"He finished his sentence at the beginning of the summer, and no one seems to have seen him since he walked out of the gate at Danbury."

"Kevin, I'm sure you recall that our friend Wulver grabbed that hecatolite spearhead right out of Iverson's hands at the Strabo benefit, in front of the top donors. I think that humiliation made him obsessed with revenge, and I doubt that prison did much to quell that. Also, as I just mentioned, he called a hit on me, targeting me as the source of his long list of problems."

"Well, from the looks of this terse note, I'd say he's back in the game."

"Agreed. We have to work under that assumption. But the wording—it's so odd. What are the days that never were? Is he just out of his mind, or is that a real thing?"

"I don't know, but since he doesn't specify *when* those days are on calendar, time is of the essence to try to figure out what the heck he means."

"And also figure out what sacred spear he's talking about. Right now Gae Bolg, the spear we brought back from Ireland, is under lock and key at Sarah Lawrence. I'll instruct security to keep it on twenty-four-hour watch."

"Artemis, my gut tells me that he wants to make a bigger splash then just getting revenge on us for the Strabo incident. I think he wants to shake up the art world."

"By going for the biggest fish out there."

"Right. The only problem is, we don't know where or even *what* that fish is."

"Kevin, let me get down to campus, and I will get to work on this."

As a tenured professor, Artemis had all-night privileges at the Sarah Lawrence library. She preferred doing intensive research when she was all alone, with her books and papers spread out on a big table among the stacks.

At the library, armed with a thermos full of hot coffee, she pulled a yellow legal pad from her backpack and began jotting down some speculative equations.

"Stolen from his hands" equals Iverson. Note: In his usual egocentric fashion, he's boasting about a crime he hasn't even pulled off yet.

Iverson equals stolen art.

Art equals a painting, a statue, an artifact. Something ancient would be typical of his taste in crime, but how ancient?

She began scrawling ideas, talking to herself in a low, library-friendly voice, even though there was no one to disturb.

"Let's see. There are hundreds of paintings that include spears, from modern times all the way back to prehistoric petroglyphs, but are there really any valuable paintings of a spear all by itself?"

She chewed lightly on her pencil.

"There are also plenty of statues, great ones, that include spears, but how would a criminal steal the spear out of the hands of a bronze or terra cotta warrior?"

She yawned. The coffee was wearing off.

"That leaves artifacts. Spears are in lots of collections. The Museum of Natural History, The British Museum. That list goes on and on."

She drained the last of the coffee and spoke again to the empty reading room.

"Okay. Let's assume for now that it's an artifact, a real spear. Even if we're right about that, we have the other, stranger mystery to solve. What and when are the nights that never were?"

The urge to sleep finally won out over the background buzz of caffeine. She crossed her arms and put her head down, "just for a minute."

CHAPTER 20

THE WAKE-UP

Thursday, October 12, 1967
Bronxville, New York

Artemis was dreaming about a secluded beach on the Amalfi Coast when she heard a familiar voice that didn't belong in Positano.

"Why, good morning, Artemis! Are we homeless these days, sleeping in the library?"

She woke with a start. Light was streaming through the clerestory windows.

"Holy cow, Professor Bainbridge! I must have fallen asleep."

"I can assure you, you're not the first distinguished scholar to have surrendered to the waves of Morpheus in this hall, using their research notes as an impromptu pillow. Voice of experience, I'm afraid. Could I ask what you're working on that kept you up all hours here on campus?"

"You might be the exact person who can help me. If you've got a few minutes before your next art history class, please have a seat and perhaps you can help me solve a mystery."

"Of course."

Artemis kept her "night job" as a secret agent discretely quiet, so she didn't give the professor any background information about Iverson or Strabo. She simply wrote out the cryptic message she had received on a fresh legal sheet and put it on the big table in front of Bainbridge. He adjusted his reading glasses on his nose and read, sometimes mouthing the words silently as he repeated his scan of the message. He finally removed his glasses, polished the lenses, and replaced them in the breast pocket of his tweed blazer.

"Well, I don't know who had a spear stolen from his hands, but I do know about the nights that never were. There were ten of them. Let me grab a volume in the history stacks and look up the correct dates, or lack thereof, to be precise."

He returned a few minutes later with a hefty volume. He blew the dust off.

"Here we go. Johnson's *Europe in the Sixteenth Century*. He wrote in the 1800s, so I daresay he was a bit closer in time to his subject than we are now. However, this incident is well known. Pope Gregory sought to replace the old Roman Julian calendar, in order to put the fall equinox on October fifteenth, so it would line up properly with the spring equinox. They should be exactly six lunar months apart, to square with the two annual solstices. To accomplish this, he had to get rid of ten days somehow. Being the pope and the absolute ruler of most of Christendom, or Europe as we call it today, he simply declared that Thursday the fourth of October 1582 would be followed immediately by Friday the fifteenth of October 1582. The intervening ten days would just disappear by papal decree. The pope can do that sort of thing, you know. The English, having just broken away from Roman authority in 1534, were averse to following papal decrees, so they dragged their feet on the issue for another hundred years. The upshot of it all, in my estimation, is that the 'nights that never were' refer to the fifth through fourteenth of October. At least, a student of history like you, me, or the author of this cryptic note might interpret it that way. Those nights would be coming up shortly, wouldn't they?"

Artemis was wide awake now.

"Of course! Yes, the author of that note is indeed an expert on European history. That must be it. Do you have time for one more mystery?"

"For a stellar student who has blossomed into a distinguished professor herself? Of course."

"The sacred spear that he threatens to steal. Is there any connection at all between the missing dates and a spear of some sort?"

Bainbridge closed his eyes and leaned his head back, as Artemis had seen him do in the classroom when pondering a thorny question. He seemed to be scanning all the books he had ever read, looking for a key word that would unlock the puzzle. He opened his eyes and nodded slowly, as if agreeing with a point he himself had made.

"I think I've got it. A strange thing happened on that October 15, 1582. If someone died at midnight on the fourth, it's still uncertain exactly what date should be assigned to their demise, since the calendar went awry for ten days at one second after midnight."

"So who died at that time who might be connected to a sacred spear?"

"Artemis, I must make my nine o'clock freshman class, but I assure you that, in the words of the bard, 'thereby hangs a tale.' Let's meet for lunch at the club, noon sharp."

CHAPTER 21

BAINBRIDGE'S THEORY

The two professors met for lunch at Bainbridge's club, Whitby Castle in Rye, not far from the campus. The nineteenth-century edifice was built in classic Gothic stone style, complete with crenelated battlements. Over simple salads, brown bread, chunks of Parmesan cheese, and, of course, coffee for Artemis and milk tea for the elder professor, the tale was spun.

"Now, Artemis, our story begins just a scant 385 years ago, which places it in the somewhat recent past for a medievalist like yourself, but bear with me. This part of the mystery blends into my own field, art history.

"Back in 1582, a Spanish Carmelite nun died. Teresa of Avila wasn't your everyday nun. She was a mystic who wrote detailed accounts of vibrant visions that she experienced. She spent years traveling and establishing monasteries all over Spain, alternating with long periods of total detachment, cloistered behind walls. There were rumors that she could perform miracles, and some claimed that they saw her levitate. Now, you recall that she died in 1582, and it just so happened that she died on either October 4 or October 15 of that year, because as you recall from our conversation this morning, Pope Gregory tossed out the Julian calendar on that exact night. Ultimately the Church assigned her feast day to the fifteenth, because Saint Francis had already laid claim to October 4."

Artemis thought back to the little figurine of Teresa of Avila in the Mexican *mercado*, the figurine that Viviana described as *brujería*, a talisman of magical power. She took a sip and put down her coffee cup.

"So that ties her in with the days that never were, or literally the dates that never were. What about the sacred spear?"

"That's what this all leads up to. I must admit I was putting this theory together in my head during class while I droned on about Rococo ornamentation. I don't think the students noticed, if they were listening at all!"

Bainbridge took a sip from his teacup and continued.

"Seventy years after Teresa's death, Gian Lorenzo Bernini was at the top rank of artists in Rome. His sculptures were passionate and lifelike, and his experience as a stage set designer made him a sort of master showman on the grand scale. He designed, for example, the massive piazza in front of Saint Peter's Basilica, where huge crowds still gather to be blessed by the pope.

"Well, he sometimes took commissions from outside the Vatican, one of which was a major project for a wealthy family, the Cornaros. They had chosen the left transept of a stunning church, *la chiesa di* Santa Maria della Vittoria, as their family crypt, and they wanted it done up in spectacular style, so their wealth and power would be noted for centuries, and indeed it has been, because they went with the best: Bernini."

Artemis looked at her watch.

"Tell me about the spear. This might be something I need to act on quickly!"

Bainbridge smiled and took a sip of tea.

"Bernini decided on a central marble statue in an elaborate setting, and he picked a theme that was not only full of passion but ended up generating quite a bit of controversy. Jogging back to the mystical Teresa for a moment, she wrote a vivid account of a visitation by an angel, who stabbed her repeatedly with a spear, causing a sort of ecstatic mix of pain and pleasure that she described as lifting her to the highest regions of religious bliss. Her account was well known, but no sculptor had depicted it in marble quite like Bernini. It was so lifelike and overflowing with emotion that it caused no end of scandal in the Roman church back then. Today it's revered as one of the masterpieces of the Baroque.

"So, cutting directly to the chase, the Bernini's marble angel is wielding a spear tipped with gold. It's part of the larger structure of the statue, which was carved from a single block of Siena marble, so I don't see it as easily removable. My guess is that your correspondent is an overimaginative crackpot casting himself as an arch-criminal."

"Professor, you might well have broken the case. You were always enlightening in the classroom, and you are equally so at lunch."

"So, are you doing a bit of extracurricular sleuthing on the side, Artemis?"

"Oh, no. Just asking for a friend."

Artemis pulled out her wallet, but Bainbridge waved her off.

"I've got a running account here. *Buona fortuna* with your Roman escapade."

CHAPTER 22

ALL ROADS LEAD TO ROME

Artemis rushed to the club's phone booth. She dropped a dime into the slot and dialed Macduff's direct line at Strabo.

"Kevin, I met today with Arthur Bainbridge, the art history professor emeritus on campus. I showed him the note, and he did some research. His theory makes sense to me."

She sketched out the basics for Macduff.

"Artemis, I buy it, too, and I agree that Iverson's fingerprints are all over this. When he graduated from Yale, his dad sent him on the grand tour: Paris, Florence, Venice, Trieste, and, of course, Rome. He knows the great works, and he knows where they are. He could have been a venerable art critic, but hubris is his middle name. He'd rather steal objets d'art than appreciate them like the rest of us."

"My guess is that he couldn't resist teasing us with a clue before the crime even happened, and he figured that by the time we cracked his code, he'd have the piece stolen and stashed away. That was his first mistake. Today is October 12. That gives us all of three days to head Iverson off at the pass. If he follows his usual modus operandi, he'll send a hired flunky to pull off the heist."

"Well, then we need to get you to Rome on the next flight out. You're on sabbatical right now, correct? Working on a book?"

"The book can wait. Ayotunde is working on her own book, so she'll take care of the house. Olorin is already traveling somewhere in Europe, doing her semester abroad. I can leave tonight."

"Go home and pack your bag. I'll put in a call to my contact at Alitalia and get you cleared to fly out tonight. I'll call you in thirty minutes with more details."

On the drive to Valhalla, Artemis puzzled over the question of how Iverson's henchman might be able to steal just the spear from a statue carved from a single block of marble. That might not be revealed until the last moment. As a world champion crossbow archer, she was trained to make cool, calm decisions under pressure, and it looked like that skill was going to come into play once more. The phone rang just as she fastened the zipper on her duffel bag.

"Kevin here. We're all set. Ten p.m. flight out of JFK, Terminal 1. You will be fast-tracked through customs. Take the train from Flumicino Airport into Roma Termino. When you get out of the station, walk two blocks to the Piazza de Republica. Make a left on the Via National, and you will see the Albergo Quirinale on your left as you come down the block. Your room is reserved on the Strabo account. Good luck, and here's hoping your friend Sherlock Holmes's hunch is correct."

"We'll find out soon enough, Kevin, and his name is Arthur Bainbridge."

"Okay, but Sherlock Holmes is easier to remember. Stay safe and keep me updated."

CHAPTER 23

THE SAGRESTANO

Friday, October 13, 1967
Rome, Italy

On her way to the airport, Artemis had stopped at the Sarah Lawrence campus library and checked out two books: Giorgio Vasari's *Lives of the Most Excellent Painters, Sculptors, and Architects*, and Alban Butler's 1750 *Lives of the Saints*. Artemis's dad raised her as a pure intellectual without any religious denomination, but that background gave her an openness to any and all belief systems. Her own recent past included encounters with werewolves, Irish folk heroes, and a goddess who transformed into a goose to rescue her on a Himalayan peak, so when Bainbridge dryly described Teresa's life, with one foot in this world and the other in a misty fourth dimension, Artemis was thinking that this was a woman she would probably get along with just fine. She wanted to find out more about her during the nine-hour flight.

The Vasari book of short biographies of Renaissance artists was written in the same time period when Bernini was completing his masterworks, ushering in the Baroque era. Artemis wanted to get caught up on that time and place during her flight to the Eternal City.

Artimis's redeye flight was uneventful, and her compressed study of religion and art kept her alert, with occasional catnaps. A veteran globetrotter, she was used to catching a few winks at odd times and places, including the Sarah Lawrence library. That time, she was dreaming of Italy. Now she was looking down on the Tyrrhenian Sea as she winged her way there. When the Boeing 707 began its descent over Sardinia, she stowed the two books in her duffel and gathered her ID papers. Flashing her passport and Strabo credentials at customs, she followed the crowd to the train platform and found a seat for the twenty-minute trip into Roma Termini, the city's central station. A ten-minute walk past the immense ruin of the Baths of Diocletian brought her to the front doors of the Albergo Quirinale.

As she put her duffel bag down at the front desk, she computed that she'd been on the move for fourteen hours, and now she was six hours ahead of New York. No time for jet lag, though. It was the morning of October 13. She had less than forty-eight hours to formulate a plan to protect a priceless work of art and hopefully apprehend a criminal in the process.

The desk clerk handed her an envelope containing the room key and a telegram from Macduff. She skipped the elevator and climbed the grand staircase, glad to be using her own muscles after being conveyed across an ocean. Once ensconced in her quarters she kicked off her shoes, opened the big window that looked out on the hotel's shady enclosed garden, and read Macduff's telegram.

Artemis unfolded the yellow paper with *Western Union* in bold letters across the top. Macduff's message was typed onto narrow strips of white paper, pasted below the letterhead.

NOON ROME TIME MEET WITH SEXTON DON ANTONIO SIDE DOOR SANTA MARIA CHURCH. CROSS VIA NATIONAL TURN LEFT VIA TORINO. WALK TWO BLOCKS TO PIAZZA DI SAN BERNARDO. CHURCH OFF TO YOUR RIGHT.

Artemis had two hours to get a bit of rest and something to eat. She decided to cover both needs with a visit to the walled garden. A mild autumn breeze was moving the leaves of the olive trees, and it was easy to forget that on the other side of the garden walls, Roman traffic was careening down busy urban streets. She sat at a table for one and ordered a half-liter of San Pellegrino *acqua de seltz* while she studied the menu. She settled on a simple Roman brunch of *cacio e pepe*—tonnarelli pasta tossed with pecorino cheese and freshly ground pepper. On the side, she sampled the chef's *cicoria ripassata*, wild chicory boiled, drained to soften the natural bitterness, then pan sautéed with salt, olive oil, and garlic.

The light meal and the soft breezes brought Artemis back to life, and she focused on the mission. The first task was done: getting to Rome overnight. The next one would be meeting with Don Antonio and seeing the sculpture for the first time.

The walk along the busy Via Torino took just a few minutes. From the Piazza di San Bernardo, she dodged relentlessly speeding traffic as she crossed the Largo di Santa Susanna, wondering if that might be the most dangerous part of her assignment. Safely on the sidewalk, she caught her breath in front of the massive green doors of the Santa Maria della Vittoria. The façade faced out on the Via Venti Settembre, the September breeze. Lovely street name, but now it was noon on Friday the thirteenth, and the clock was counting down thirty-six hours until midnight at the start of Sunday the fifteenth, when Bainbridge's theory and her crimefighting acumen would be tested. Prep time was in short supply, and she had to make the most of it.

She found the iron gate leading to the side door of the church. It was open. She pushed it aside and rang the doorbell. After a few sounds suggesting an interior struggle with the deadbolt, a rotund figure dressed in a black cassock appeared.

"*Saluto*! You are Artemis Fletcher from New York, yes?"

"And you must be Don Antonio."

"Indeed. That is not Don as in Donald. It's the title here in Rome for a priest, just like *father* in the States. I am the *sagrestano* of *la chiesa di* Santa Maria della Vittoria. You can just call me the sexton. I celebrate the Mass and hear confessions, but I am also charged with managing the upkeep of the building. Like a super in New York City!"

Artemis raised an eyebrow.

"Don Antonio, may I say that your English is perfect. Do I detect a slight Brooklyn accent?"

"I first learned English here in Rome, in *scuola primaria*, but I learned American, if you will, when I was assigned to the Basilica of Saint James in Brooklyn for two years, right out of the seminary. There is a long history of immigrants learning to speak American in Brooklyn, is that not so? But let's get down to the day's business. I was contacted yesterday by Kevin Macduff. The Strabo Society has had dealings, many aboveboard and many in secret, with the clergy here in Rome. We have helped them in the past, and I am glad to continue the warm relationship. Allow me to guide you while we tour the nave and the transepts. I must warn you that, since it's your first visit to the *chiesa*, you might find the ambience a bit, shall we say, distracting?"

Don Antonio swung open the side door of the church and beckoned for her to enter first. Artemis stepped in and caught her breath as she spiraled into a state of stimulus overload. Every surface seemed to be covered in multicolored marble and gold, interrupted only by massive murals and gilt-framed paintings. Everything was on a superhuman scale. They walked slowly down the center of the nave. The church was cross shaped, with elaborately decorated chapels extending to the sides. Artemis felt like she was tiny, the size of Alice in Wonderland after biting the mushroom, walking through a giant treasure chest. Don Antonio waited while she stood in silence for a few minutes, taking it all in and slowly regaining her composure.

"Artemis, the church was originally intended as a chapel for the Carmelite nuns, but while it was going up, the Romans scored a victory near Prague, and in a tradition dating all the way back to the ancients, it was decided to celebrate in a big way. Hence the church's name, Our Lady of Victory. Speaking of Carmelite nuns, the most famous one of all is celebrated here. Let's walk down toward the main altar."

They walked slowly. Everywhere Artemis looked, there seemed to be another masterpiece that would have been the center of attention anywhere else. Though Don Antonio spoke quietly, his words nonetheless echoed off the vaulted ceiling.

"In the 1500s a wealthy family could, to use a modern term, lease part of a church for use as their burial crypt. Thus, there would be side chapels, and even entire transepts, those areas that extend like the cross bars of a crucifix, that would be open to worshippers but dedicated to a specific family. One such family was the Cornaros. They chose the left transept and commissioned Bernini, who usually worked under the pope, to create a monument to the most revered Carmelite nun."

Artemis nodded, still gaping at the profusion of art and marble. She finished his thought. "Teresa of Avila."

"That's right. The mystic. Now, Bernini was not only a brilliant sculptor and architect. He was also a celebrated theatrical set designer, and he pulled out all the stops, if you'll pardon the church-organ pun. Here we are. Look to the left."

Once again, Artemis caught her breath as she felt the disorienting spiral. She was gazing at a vision in marble. The saint was reclining on a cloud, obviously not any place on earth. Standing over her was a cherub, smiling blissfully as he plunged his spear toward her. Teresa's facial expression was neither blissful nor terrified. It was simply ecstatic, not of this world. Bernini somehow created a real person floating in an out-of-body experience, out of a solid block of stone. Above the pair, golden rays shone down, mixing with actual rays of sunshine from a window hidden from the viewer, high above. The overall effect was more than a sculpture; it was an autonomous environment, and it was breathtaking not only for the craft but for the transcendent atmosphere that permeated the enclosed transept. It seemed to Artemis that an ongoing mystical experience was happening in another universe from the main nave, just steps away. Artemis thought back to the temple of Kumari Devi in Katmandu, where the little goddess morphed into other shapes and spoke to her while the incense burned. In the midst of the lush, intoxicating grandeur, a vision of another kind came into her mind's eye, the toylike little figurine of Teresa in Mexico, and Viviana's words: "We often invoke her in a magical way…She embodies our spirit of independence and our belief in a personal vision quest."

Don Antonio waited patiently until Artemis appeared ready to converse again.

"The structure over the central figures is called an *aedicule*. It represents a small temple that separates this piece from the rest of the church, like a miniature church within the church. Notice the sculpted cherubs looking down approvingly on our *bellissima* Teresa's moment of spiritual ecstasy."

Artemis pulled herself together enough to survey the setting as a potential crime scene. There was a spear all right, but it was carved, like the two main figures, from the single massive block of stone. It couldn't be pulled from the angel's hand. She had a moment of doubt. Did she make the wrong call? Was Iverson stealing another precious spear somewhere across the globe? She steeled herself. Growing up in the world of competitive archery, she learned early on to dispel any doubt after all possible preparation had been made. She was here to carry out that preparation, not indulge in a game of indecision. Don Antonio gently interrupted her reflection.

"If we look to the right and left, we see one of the most interesting facets of this entire setting. I call it a setting, rather than simply a sculpture, because Bernini, as a man of the theatre, created a theatrical scene, complete with not only characters but an audience as well! Look up, and to the right and left."

Artemis was startled to see figures looking down at the scene unfolding on the cloud. Life size, and lifelike except for being sculpted of pure white marble, four bearded men looked down from theater boxes on either side of the *aedicula*. Unlike the ecstatic main figures below them, they looked like normal, interested theatergoers. Two of them were even commenting on the activity onstage.

"One of the stipulations of Bernini's commission was the inclusion of the Cornaro patrons in the overall scheme. That's Frederico there. He was a cardinal. Over there is Giovanni looking down. Their faces, clothing, and even their beards are realistically preserved for us three centuries later. In that way, although they are buried beneath the floor, they have a kind of artistic immortality."

A bell rang, somewhere high above them.

"Now I must attend to my priestly duties. Confession is held at one p.m. This is a busy weekend here. Sunday is Santa Teresa's feast, so Mass will be filled with her devotees. Is there anything further I can do to assist in your Strabo business?"

"Yes, I would request access to this area starting at nightfall tomorrow. Tell me one more thing, please. Are the galleries where the Cornaros look down accessible from below?"

"Each gallery has a narrow stairway hidden within the church walls. I will show you how to access them before I make my way back to the sacristy."

CHAPTER 24

LA SARTORIA

Hiking back to the hotel, Artemis weighed her options. What was needed was a stakeout. If her hunch that the hit would happen at midnight on the following night was correct, she would need to be hidden somewhere in the church, out of sight but close enough to prevent whatever kind of harm might be intended for the statue. Her interest in Teresa had grown into a protective sense of loyalty, not just for the marble statue, but for the mysterious woman herself, who was so much like the lycanthropes and mystics that Artemis had known as kindred spirits, creatures of this world but not always so, with one foot in Hamlet's undiscovered country. The saint, depicted in total vulnerability, was in Artemis's care for the next forty-eight hours.

She checked for messages at the front desk. Nothing from Macduff. He would be waiting for word from her since it was up to her to improvise this mission. The desk clerk addressed her in English.

"*Signorina*, would you like for me to inform you about restaurants, entertainment venues, museums in the local area? We have many diversions and places of historical interest."

"Oh, I'm working. I'm not really a *tourista*."

"I see. However, if you want to view a marvelous façade right next door, we are directly adjacent to the opera house, the Teatro dell'Opera di Roma. Sadly, the season doesn't begin until next month, but the piazza and the building itself are worth a short walk."

Wanting to respond politely to his graciousness, she answered in a friendly tone.

"I really don't have time. Work…*lavoro*."

"Of course. Hopefully you will stay with us someday during the season. The hotel has a door that leads directly into the opera house. Our patrons have no need to even venture outside during the winter months."

"Thank you for the suggestion. *Grazie*. I hope to do that someday."

"*Prego. Buonasera.*"

Artemis was halfway up the grand stairway when she stopped, fixated on a sudden inspiration. She hurried back to the front desk.

"*Per favore*, is it possible to send a telegram from here?"

"Of course, *signorina*. We have a Western Union office right here in the hotel. The business office is on the mezzanine. I will call up and tell them you are on your way."

"*Grazie.*"

"*Prego.*"

Artemis wrote a short message in longhand and gave it to the telegraph operator.

KEVIN. NEED IMMEDIATE ACCESS TO TEATRO DELL'OPERA DI ROMA COSTUME DEPARTMENT.

The next thirty minutes seemed like hours as she felt time ticking down to midnight on Saturday night. Finally, the telegraph operator handed her the yellow sheet.

ACCESS GRANTED. THEATRE CLOSED BUT COSTUME SHOP OPEN DURING REHEARSALS. USE HOTEL DIRECT DOOR.

Artemis was led to the door by a bellman, who knocked in a sort of Morse code, and stepped aside as the door opened into a dimly lit hallway. A young woman emerged from the shadow.

"You are Strabo?"

"Yes."

"Come with me, please."

Their path led them past the wings leading out to the stage, where Artemis heard a heroic tenor singing, accompanied by a pianist who stopped at certain points and shouted directions in Italian. She was led up narrow stairs lit only by hanging light bulbs, deliberately dimmed so as not to dilute the stage lighting below. The young lady led the way to a brightly lit, large studio. She bowed and disappeared down the narrow stairs. A red-haired man rushed toward Artemis; his hand extended to shake hers.

"*Ciao! Ciao!* You are Artemis Fletcher, no? *Che figatta!* How great that you are here!"

He was the kind of man often described as barrel chested, and if his chest was a barrel, his head was a cask. Those two characteristics no doubt contributed to his booming baritone voice. His enthusiasm was instantly disarming.

"Yes. That's me. Strabo must have…"

He cut her off with a wave of his hand.

"Oh yes, yes. They are all business. You are in *la sartoria* now. We are all about magic."

"Well, I have a request."

"Of course, a request. But first. Look around you. This is a place of magic."

He lowered his voice to a *sotto voce* whisper.

"We have sixty thousand stage costumes in our collection."

His volume went back up, *subito forte*.

"Sixty thousand! Going back to the 1860s. We can costume any opera in the repertoire. Look around you. We are always busy creating. I am the boss, but I am a very easy boss. My people..." He gestured broadly at a dozen young people cutting, sewing, ironing, drawing on large draft easels. "My people are the best. Today, though, we make only peasant costumes. Many peasant costumes. Too many peasant costumes! *Il Trovatore* opens the season in a few weeks, and we must be ready to dress the peasants. Of course, I reserve the troubadour's colorful costume for myself. I am the boss!"

He seemed to be in a constant state of celebration.

"Oh please. I beg your forgiveness, *signorina*. I have neglected to introduce myself. I am Matteo Sapelli. I took the name Sapelli in honor of our first and greatest costume designer, Luigi Sapelli. But enough about me for the moment. What is it you need from us here in *la sartoria*?"

"I need to become a statue."

"A statue! *Meravigliosa*! How wonderful! Tell me, is it for a masked ball? All Saints' Day?"

"Not exactly, but I do need a costume for an event."

"*Che figata*! And when is it that you need to be a statue?"

"Tomorrow night."

"Tomorrow night! It's your good fortune that you have come to the greatest *sartoria* in Italy. No doubt you inspected the *sartoria* in Florence and Milan and found them wanting." He laughed heartily.

"Matteo, I know you are busy preparing for the season."

"Preparing what? Peasant costumes! Tell me, of what is this statue made?"

"Marble. Pure white Siena marble."

He stroked his chin thoughtfully.

"And are you a man or a woman statue?"

"A man. A bearded man."

He laughed again, even louder this time.

"And you are an *Italian* man?"

"Yes. A Roman."

"Ah, a bearded Roman. Hadrian?"

"No, a Roman from the 1600s. A Cornaro."

"A Cornaro. *Mamma mia*! You will be *molto ricco*, a very rich man!"

Matteo stroked his chin again, momentarily lost in thought.

"We can do this. First, you must meet my assistant. She is here for the month of *ottobre*, helping us launch the opera season. I tell you; she is talented beyond her years. Her skill at producing lifelike faces is unsurpassed. If anyone can turn a blond-haired American woman into a bearded old Cornaro, I believe that she can. Let me introduce her to you. *Assistente! Assistente!*"

Matteo's office door opened, and Artemis's jaw nearly dropped to the floor of the *sartoria*.

CHAPTER 25

THE ASSISTANT

"Olorin?"

"Artemis!"

"*You* are the assistant with the prodigious talent for faces? Of course! You trained yourself back home!"

"In Nigeria, in the sacred grove of Osun. I had to teach myself."

"Then you were a good student and a good teacher as well! But what are you doing here at the Rome opera house?"

"It's part of my semester abroad. My faculty adviser at Sarah Lawrence made arrangements for me to intern under Matteo and learn from him."

Matteo did a stage-worthy double take.

"*Signorina*, I must correct that statement. I am learning from her!"

He grew momentarily serious.

"African masks have been a huge influence on European artists, ever since the Paris Exhibition in 1890. Picasso copied them and called them cubist portraits! This young lady is *la verisma*, the real deal, as you say in the States. It is a privilege to have her here with us. Now, to business. Tell her everything you told me, Artemis Fletcher."

Matteo returned to the big studio, bellowing at his interns, while the two women huddled.

As the shadows were growing long over the Piazza Beniamino Gigli, Artemis and Olorin completed their plans upstairs inside the opera house. They emerged from the office to find the last of the assistants shutting down their sewing machines and heading home for the day. Matteo greeted them in his trademark warm fashion.

"Talented *signorinas*! How has your plan progressed?"

Artemis nodded to Olorin, who was politely waiting to let the elder woman speak first.

"Artemis and I are prepared to execute the plan. I will need to have access to the studio overnight."

"Granted!"

"Artemis will return in the early morning, after her coffee, if I recall her daily regimen. Then we will proceed."

"Bravo! Well done, Olorin."

"Matteo, I hope this question is not impertinent, but aren't you curious why Artemis needs to become a bearded man from a Baroque Roman family?"

"Whether I am curious or not is unimportant."

He pointed a thumb in Artemis's direction.

"Olorin, this woman is from the Strabo Society. Since you are her friend, I might guess that you are from Strabo as well, but guessing and curiosity are not favorable traits when one works with Strabo. Over the years, the Rome opera has provided Strabo with costumes, actors, and intelligence information. It's amazing what one overhears in an opera house dressing room. In turn,

Strabo supports us in a spirit of generosity. However, the tacit agreement is no questions asked, *capiche*?"

Artemis stepped into the conversation.

"Matteo, tell me. Have you ever been enlisted to take part in a Strabo operation?"

"You know that I can't answer that, but…" He grinned. "If it's something interesting…" He drew out the dramatic pause. "By all means, yes!"

"Okay then, consider yourself part of the team. If the staff have all gone home, we will fill you in on your role."

"I am ready to study for my part!"

For the next thirty minutes, as the big windows grew dark, the two women filled Matteo in on the mission. Artemis finally stood up, a bit groggy after two full days with no real sleep.

"I'm going to head up to my room and get some rest before we execute the operation tomorrow."

Olorin reminded her to arrive early, before the staff would be at work.

Matteo, warming to what he saw as his upcoming heroic role, boomed in a *forte voce*.

"*Domani*! But first, a toast to our success!"

He drew a bottle of red wine from his file cabinet, along with three wineglasses.

"Chianti Classico, 1961. One of the great Tuscany vintages! This one will remind you of tart fruit, like our *amerina* cherries that come in the little jug."

Olorin politely begged off. Her Yoruba faith forbade alcohol consumption, and she was looking forward to a full night of work. Artemis took a sip and bade her teammates goodnight.

Matteo drained his glass and sighed with contentment. Designing costumes was great, but a bit of espionage was even better.

CHAPTER 26

THE MASK

Saturday, October 14, 1967

At six a.m. sharp, Artemis knocked on the hotel door that led directly backstage at the opera. She had memorized the knock that her escort used on the previous day. It worked. The same young woman, dressed in black, opened the door and silently escorted Artemis up the labyrinthian stairways to the *sartoria*. Olorin was dozing on a makeup artist's rotating chair, positioned at a large worktable where three newly stitched, white neck-to-toe coveralls were laid out. Adjacent to the table was a large stove. The flame was turned off, and a large cauldron was cooling, filled with what looked like five gallons of cream of wheat. Several white wigs, of the kind that male actors might wear in *The Marriage of Figaro*, lay on the worktable, along with a pair of shears. Taped to the wall above the table was a poster for the upcoming season premiere, *Il Trovatore*, featuring a large photo of the composer, Giuseppe Verdi. He lived into his eighties, and he always sported a bushy but neatly trimmed beard, with a flowing mustache. That trademark accoutrement turned pure white in his advanced years.

The props were in place. Only a few details remained to set their trap, and for those the two operatives had to take a morning hike.

"Olorin, wake up! We'll be late!"

The younger woman rubbed her eyes.

"Late for what?"

"Why, Mass, of course!"

In the early morning October chill, the agnostic intellectual and the Yoruba adherent straggled up the Via Torino and found a vacant pew just before Don Antonio intoned "*In nomine Patris…*" During the ceremony, Olorin studied the Cornaro figures from her viewpoint down below the galleries. She made detailed sketches of their faces, visible clothing, and beards. Artemis, without drawing attention, scanned the luxurious surroundings as sunlight began streaming through stained glass and hidden ceiling lenses that focused on individual statues, enhancing their lifelike appearance. As the ceremony progressed, she was able, from her pew, to sketch a map of the important landmarks, obstacles, and possible escape routes. By the time Don Antonio uttered "*Ite, missa est,*" dismissing the faithful, they had each gathered the information they would need later that night.

After doffing his chasuble cloak and dismissing the two altar boys, Don Antonio joined them in the nave.

"Do you have everything you need?"

"Hopefully, yes. The main doors will be locked, correct?"

"They have been barred for decades. The good Lord himself would be hard pressed to try to open them."

"So, the only way in and out tonight will be the side door on the right transept, opposite the Bernini? Can you leave that closed but unlocked?"

"After the four p.m. vigil Mass, and then an hour of confessions at five, I'll be returning for the night to the rectory next door. I will leave that door unlocked at six p.m., sundown, under your watch."

"Excellent. Then I believe we are prepared, Don Antonio."

"Artemis, just one more thing, *per favore*."

He fidgeted nervously.

"Our *bellissima* Teresa is in no danger of being damaged, is she? Tomorrow morning is the Sunday Mass celebrating her annual feast, and her devotees will fill the pews. If anything should happen to her during the night…"

His voice trailed off. Artemis wanted to pat him on the arm in an encouraging way, but she didn't know if one did that to a priest.

"Don Antonio, I can guarantee you that no harm will come to the saint."

Of course, she couldn't guarantee that at all, but the poor man was so distraught that she just wanted to comfort him.

"You've been fasting all morning, Don Antonio. Have some breakfast and leave the saint in our care."

The two women repaired back to the opera house to put the finishing touches on their costume design.

Olorin directed the interns to move her materials to the back studio, where the door could be shut, and the conspirators could work without disturbance. Two baritones were required to lug the cauldron and the revolving makeup chair. Nothing alerted the staff that anything unusual might be brewing, since powdered wigs, false beards, and cauldrons full of strange concoctions were normal ingredients *del giorno* in *la sartoria*.

Olorin had fitted herself for her coveralls, wig, and beard during the night. She used her artist's mind's eye to rough in the sizes for Artemis and Matteo, and now she did the final fitting, basting, and stitching. Next, she fitted them with their powdered wigs and beards. Then she draped them in lavish robes, courtesy of the props department and her pair of sharp shears. Studying her sketches from morning Mass, she was able to create three newly minted Cornaro brothers, who could fit right in with Bernini's renditions, without being exact copies.

At three o'clock, Artemis ducked out for a quick meeting at Roma central police headquarters, just two blocks away. She was back by four, and they finalized plans. There was one logistical hurdle to leap: The cauldron of cornstarch and zinc oxide mixed with water was too bulky and heavy to heft all the way to the church. The time had come to dress and brush the mixture on from head to toe.

Wigs, beards, robes, hands, and faces all had to be the color and visual texture of marble. Olorin had done several experiments to make sure that the mixture wasn't so rich that when it dried, they would turn into stiff mummies. It wouldn't do to helplessly watch a thief at work from the gallery, unable to move in a full-body plaster cast. She had spent the night thinning the mixture to the point where it would mold into place and stay without stiffening or dripping. At least, that was the hope.

Once they were suited and brushed down with the clown white, they alternated sitting and standing while the formula dried. Matteo looked at himself in the mirror.

"Bravo! Bello!"

Even the seasoned interns were a bit surprised to see three sixteenth-century grandees emerge from the back studio and start slowly, ever so slowly, down the rickety backstage stairs. Once on level ground, they clustered in the shadow of the marquee while a stagehand hailed a taxi. When the first cabbie stopped, the three white figures came running toward his vehicle. He took one look and roared off, making the sign of the cross. A second cab stopped, and the cabbie took a more sardonic view of things. Matteo could only fit in the front passenger seat, and he was the only one of the three who spoke Italian, so he carried on a terse conversation initiated by the driver.

"*Tre pagliacci? e Leoncavallo stasera?*"

"*No pagliacci. Statues. La chiesa di Santa Maria della Vittoria, per favore!*"

"*Vittoria! Non ci sono gia abbastanza li?*"

"*No. Esse bisogno altri tre.*"

In the back seat, Olorin cast an inquisitive glance at Artemis, her white-bearded companion, who shrugged. Apparently whatever Matteo said had satisfied the cabbie's curiosity. They rode the rest of the way in silence.

CHAPTER 27

THE VIGIL

Darkness had fallen when they arrived at the side door. The church was empty and silent, with only a scattering of dim night lights on, high above them in the vault. Artemis signaled for silence as they made their way across the nave and stood beneath the right-side gallery of the transept. She pressed on a wooden panel near the floorboard, and a narrow door opened in the wall. She signaled to continue being silent and pointed across the transept. Once inside, she pressed another panel and, to a viewer outside, the door disappeared once more.

Before departing the theater, Matteo had equipped Artemis and Olorin each with gilded lengths of rope, which had been stored in the *Pirates of Penzance* locker. The pirate king used those to make his stage entrance, swinging down from the ship's rigging. In this case, the rigging was the Ionic columns that lined the back of the galleries where the two agents would be hiding in plain sight, ready to swing down and pounce on a moment's notice.

Olorin and Matteo found the secret panel on the left wall, and Olorin squeezed in, with the rope coiled over her left shoulder. Matteo balked. Although Olorin, tiny as she was, was supposed to squeeze through the door designed for Italians of sixteenth-century size, there was no way he could fit through. A bit crestfallen, he signaled for Olorin to continue up to the gallery. As he shuffled disconsolately across the nave, it occurred to him that the priest's confessional booth would make an ideal hiding place. It might be a while, hours perhaps, before the thief showed up, and the priest's booth had a comfortable seat, while the penitent's booth was furnished only with a hard kneeler. He chose the first booth, claiming the right of possession on the assumption that Don Antonio was finished with his priestly duties for the night.

Time passed slowly in the silent church. Artemis made sure to keep her luminous wristwatch hidden beneath her cloak, but she stole a glance occasionally. Her guess was that the hit would come at midnight, since that's when the missing days came to an end and the day after would commence, but she had no way to predict how far in advance the perpetrator would come to case the place and prepare to steal the spear. She still didn't know what that might entail, or how many confederates there might be.

To pass the time, she used the silent centering meditation techniques that served her well back in her competitive crossbow days, but she couldn't resist a train of thought that had lately become recurrent. Her memory went back to her kidnapping at Caffe Regio in Greenwich Village. Her distracted inspection of a cappuccino machine was a rookie mistake. Then there was the swordfight with the mad professor in Ireland, when Tunde came to her rescue in a flash of resourceful instinct. Sure, there was the Japanese temple incident, when she called up the resolve and ironclad focus of her younger days, but then there was the off-balance crossbow shot on the Kensico Dam that almost brought her career literally crashing down. Mistakes like that might be written off as moments of inattention in normal life, but her life had never been normal. Was all this somehow connected to the dreams in Mexico?

As she waited in the darkness to confront another criminal, she screwed her courage to the sticking place and glanced again at her watch. It was almost midnight.

Olorin, meanwhile, having grown up the child of a hunting culture in the African forest, was well adapted to sitting silently for long periods of time, waiting for prey to appear. She was relaxed and smiled at the idea that she was probably the first visitor to chant softly to the Yoruba *orishas* for help and guidance in that massive Catholic edifice.

Matteo was comfortable on his priestly chair. His flowing robe had enabled him to smuggle the remainder of yesterday's chianti into the church, and he was looking forward to a bit of swashbuckling adventure later in the evening.

The old building settled back into its silent role as the protector of Bernini's priceless treasure.

CHAPTER 28

CONVERGENCE

Jimmy the Blade shifted uncomfortably on his bare mattress. Iverson had provided him with a room in Rome. That was the deal, but the room turned out to be a utility closet in the basement of a rundown flophouse near the industrial end of the train station. Jimmy was also learning about jet lag. The nine-hour plane trip from Queens was not like taking the subway from Rockaway to Union Square. After two days, he was still sleeping odd hours, waking up whenever another train rumbled by, shaking the building.

Still, the job had gone okay so far. He found his contact, a fence who dealt in stolen goods, and picked up the tools he would need. In a canvas army surplus duffel, he had the diamond-blade saw, which he would ditch after the job, and a cardboard tube containing a rolled-up tourist poster of the Coliseum, Pantheon, and so on. He hadn't actually seen any of that stuff, but if his luck held out, the poster would conceal the spear from customs. He also picked up a bottle of seltzer to lubricate the diamond blade while he sawed through the marble.

Iverson had provided walking directions from the train station to the church. Jimmy started out at sundown, stopping at a restaurant along the way to blow some of his advance money. Looking at the menu, he didn't see anything that looked like Italian food to him. Zucchini flowers. Who eats that? No spaghetti, lasagna, or even a slice of pizza! Italy was a disappointment. He couldn't wait to do the job and get back to Brooklyn with a fresh bankroll.

After eating whatever it was and downing a few glasses of table wine, he continued onward to the church. Iverson had told him to forget about the big front doors and go straight around to the side door on the right. He tried the iron gate. It was unlocked. The church door was unlocked, too. This was easy money! Jimmy pushed the door open and entered, dragging the duffel bag.

As his eyes became used to the semi-darkness, he stood stock still, awestruck. This wasn't Saint Mary, Star of the Sea in Brooklyn. This wasn't like any church, or anything at all, that he'd ever seen. He stood for a long time in the center aisle. The wine was taking effect, and he got a sense that eyes were looking at him from every direction. There were statues, huge paintings, even vaults that looked like coffins everywhere he turned. Then he saw the angel with the spear and he remembered the job. He approached the statue slowly, like it was a living thing that might attack him. He looked up. There was a weird balcony built right into the wall, with five men who were looking straight down at him. He moved back and looked again. He was certain that their eyes were following him. One of them seemed to turn his head, tracking him. He turned to the left and saw five more ghostly men, with the same eyes that seemed to move. Jimmy the Blade started trembling. He tried to think straight, but his knees felt weak. He muttered shakily to himself.

"This place gives me the creeps!"

Even though he spoke in a near whisper, his voice echoed off the vault high above and ricocheted around the vast room, mocking him.

To steady himself, he repeated Iverson's deal out loud.

"Five in advance, five on completion."

Jimmy set his jaw, took a deep breath, and made one more announcement, to what he believed was the empty church.

"Okay, Iverson, let's get your spear."

Jimmy had no idea that there might be anyone within earshot, especially someone who might recognize his Brooklyn accent or the name Iverson. His self-directed pep talk emboldened him to move forward and search for a way to scale the platform where the statue rested. From there he could figure out how to climb onto it and get a kerf cut into the marble spear. Then it would be a matter of dousing the groove with water and keeping the cut clean, working the cutting edge back and forth. He dragged a chair from behind the altar. Nice red velvet cushion: the kind of thing a bishop would sit on, or maybe Cardinal Spellman. Standing on the cushion, he was able to hoist himself up next to the statue and wrap one arm around the angel's legs.

While he was slowly pulling himself up with one arm and dragging the duffel bag with the other, Jimmy made a mistake. He glanced back up at the balcony where the ghostly men stared down at him. He was doubly certain that one of them had real eyes, eyes that followed him. He froze for a long time, unwilling to back down, but unable to drag himself up. He closed his eyes to shut out the vision of the white ghosts and, breathing deeply, pulled himself up high enough to stand on the platform next to the statue. Now he could spray some seltzer on the spear and get a kerf cut started.

He shook the seltzer bottle and sprayed. Then he put it down on the nearest flat surface, part of the statue's robe. He lifted the saw into position, and that's when all hell broke loose.

A beam of light hit Jimmy in the eyes, blinding him. A voice shouted at him in English.

"Hold it right there! Drop that saw!"

Jimmy was too frightened to make sense of it. The voice was coming from the gallery, from the ghost men. The light went out, and he looked up, just in time for one of the ghosts to swing down on a rope and hit him square in the solar plexus. With the wind knocked out of him, he slid off the statue. His handsaw went rattling into the darkness, and the seltzer bottle sprayed him as he hit the platform, skidded across the slick marble, and fell to the church floor. Dazed, he opened his eyes to see another ghost man swing down from the other side.

The job was blown. His only shot was to find a way to get out of there in one piece and get to the train station. For a moment, he thought in terror of Iverson's last words to him: Don't screw up. He'd screwed up, now he had to make tracks somewhere, out of this place of ghosts.

He raised his head and remembered the door where he came in. If he could reach that...He got up and glanced back at the statue. The two ghosts who swung down on ropes looked like they were having a tough time running after him. Their legs were stiff like mummies. Maybe he could make a mad dash for the door. He crossed in front of the main altar, sliding on the polished stone but keeping his footing. He didn't look back at the ghosts. He kept his eyes on the door. Thirty feet, twenty feet... His legs were working now. He was running on pure adrenaline. Ten more feet and he'd be free. As he passed the bank of confessionals, the priest's booth suddenly burst open and *another* ghost, this one a giant, bolted out, roaring in Italian. The monster leapt on Jimmy and flattened him to the cold marble floor. Jimmy the Blade, curled up like a baby, trembled in terror.

The giant stood over him and beat on his chest, singing in a monstrous voice.

"Tale e fine del malfattore!"

The other two ghosts hobbled over and stood stiffly over Jimmy. The church door opened, admitting a dozen *politzia di stato*. Jimmy, still trembling, was led outside to the Roman rolling cell, which then roared off into the night.

In the morning, Saint Teresa's devotees would have no idea that anything unusual at all had transpired during the night. Don Antonio, arriving early to turn on the lights and dust off the statues, would notice a spray of San Pellegrino on the angel's spear. He would wipe that dry and continue his preparations for Saint Teresa's Mass.

CHAPTER 29

THE FEAST OF SAINT TERESA

Sunday, October 15, 1967
Rome, Italy

It was a lovely autumn day on the Viminal Hill. Seated around a wrought-iron table in the Quirinale's walled garden, Artemis, Olorin, and Matteo compared notes on their midnight adventure.

"Artemis, I guess I didn't factor in three hours of sitting still while the whitewash dried. It took me half the night to make my face recognizable, even to myself!"

"Olorin, the worst part was finding out that we could barely move once we swung down. He could have darted right out the door if it wasn't for Matteo coming out of his confessional booth like a raging bull."

"All in the work of a day, *me amiche*. I often boast that I could have played the giant ghost in Mozart's *Don Giovanni* without using stilts!"

"By the way, Matteo, what exactly did you say to our cab driver that made him stop asking questions?"

"Oh, he asked if we were clowns." Matteo laughed in his *forte* baritone. "I told him no; we were statues going to the *chiesa* della Vittoria. He cried out, 'They don't have enough statues there already?' and I said, 'No, they need three more!' That seemed to satisfy him."

"Ah, very clever, but what was it you sang so triumphantly while you stood over the terrified crook last night, vaunting and pounding your chest?"

"Oh, that. It was from the closing scene of *Don Giovanni*, when the giant ghost drags the villain down to hell. The chorus closes the show, singing, 'Such is the end of the evildoer!'"

"Excellent! Olorin, when I get back to New York, I will report to Macduff that you coordinated this mission, a mission that saved a priceless work of art from desecration, and Matteo, it's truly been a pleasure. I hope we get to work together again."

"Artemis, just think of me as your Italian Giacomo Bond!"

There was time for one more toast all around, and then Artemis headed for the train to take her to the airport and from there, home. There would be much to recount to Tunde, including teaming up with fledgling crimefighter Olorin, and there was also much to mull over in her own mind, after encountering the mystical Teresa of Avila on two far-flung continents.

PART FOUR

Stealing Strabo

CHAPTER 30

THE NAMESAKE

Monday, October 23, 1967
Sarah Lawrence College, Bronxville, New York

The classroom bell rang.

Artemis Fletcher, on sabbatical from her teaching job at Sarah Lawrence College and refreshed from a week's rest after her Roman adventure, had volunteered to substitute for Professor Bainbridge while he was recuperating from surgery. Artemis was looking forward to enlightening Bainbridge's students on a bit of literary history.

"My topic today is the geographer Strabo and an exciting new technology. That is, 'new' if you happened to be a college student in 45 BC. Has anyone in the class ever heard of the Strabo Society?"

As she expected, only a few hands went up.

"Well, I'm a member, and today I want to tell you a little bit about the real Strabo, and how his education, two thousand years ago, was in many ways much like yours.

"He was born around 60 BC in Asia Minor, or what we now know as Turkey. He was a Roman citizen of the empire. When he was your age, he traveled to the legendary library of Alexandria in Egypt, where he spent five years studying at the ancient world's greatest repository of knowledge. It was there that he encountered a groundbreaking new technology, the codex. Did you ever wonder what books an ancient student might read, or if in fact there were books at all back then?

"Up until that time, a library was a place that housed papyrus scrolls. They were rolled up and fragile, hard to store and hard to find on a shelf. A new technology, called the codex, developed by the Romans, changed all of that. They used separate pages that could be written on both sides, so access to individual passages, like our modern chapters, became easy. In addition, the pages were all bound together on the left side, creating a durable spine, and solid back and front covers could be bound as well, so the codex included its own protective shell during storage and transport. Does this sound familiar?"

A hand went up.

"It sounds like a book!"

"Precisely. The easiest way to understand a codex is simply to look at one of your textbooks. They are indeed codices, although the term is generally used for ancient and medieval volumes. One interesting footnote to all of this is a variation called the palimpsest. That's an ancient Roman page that was written over in the Christian era. For example, there is a page of Strabo's geography book written in his era that was scratched out four hundred years later and written over with part of the New Testament. Palimpsests keep literary scholars busy trying to decipher that bottom layer!

"Now back to our friend Strabo. After his five years of study, he traveled the world around the Mediterranean. He drew a map of that world as he knew it, and around 9 BC he published seventeen volumes of what he called *Geographica*. Copies circulated around Europe in the Middle Ages, even into the Renaissance. Columbus, for example, studied it when he was planning his 1492 voyage, looking for a sea route to the Far East. Neither he nor ancient Strabo knew, of course, that a continent lay between Europe and China, but Strabo still wears the title of Western civilization's first geographer. Nowadays, medieval era copies of his work are rare, priceless museum pieces. If you come across one at a tag sale, let me know!"

The classroom bell rang again.

"It looks like we're out of time. Pack up your codices! Professor Bainbridge will be back on Thursday."

CHAPTER 31

THE LATE DELIVERY

Tuesday, October 24, 1967
Southampton, New York

Hugo Van Elland was fuming. He glared at his desk calendar as if it, all by itself, was the cause of his mounting anger. In a way, it was. October was disappearing fast, and a delivery that was promised on the eighteenth of the month was six days late. Why did he trust that idiot Iverson? He was supposed to have the spear in hand by the sixteenth, and the deal was that it would be in Van Elland's hands by the eighteenth. Now it was the twenty-fourth, and no spear. In Van Elland's business, late deliveries were not good. Not good at all. Not good for him, and not good for whoever was supposed to keep their word.

Van Elland had been in the game for years. He had a basement, a backyard shed, and a detached garage filled with black-market art, but his obsession was never satisfied. To Van Elland, the stupid spear that hadn't shown up was unimportant. He just needed it as collateral to trigger the real deal, the deal of his lifetime. He'd become fixated on acquiring, by any means, all four of Van Gogh's preparatory sketches for *The Langlois Bridge*. That was the jewel he needed to complete his crown. It would be a complex job. The infernal spear, Iverson's bright idea, was only the beginning. The four Van Gogh sketches were housed in distant locations. That meant four different jobs.

The German piece of the puzzle, the sketch in the Staatsgalleri Stuttgart, was the crucial first step. That one was done. Van Elland had discretely retained a skilled larcenist who worked in the national gallery's archive. The sketch was warehoused on the dockside in Hamburg and would be stowed on the *Hanseatic II's* maiden voyage, due to arrive in New York on Christmas Eve. With that in hand, acquiring the LA County and Rhode Island sketches would be a simple matter of hiring the right talent. The Morgan library sketch? Why, Van Elland might even pull that one off himself! He chuckled at the thought. Feeling celebratory, he yanked a bottle from the bottom drawer of his desk, poured a shot of Stroopwaffel liqueur and downed it.

Van Elland was looking forward to a very merry Christmas, with all four of the sketches stored in his basement vault. He considered Van Gogh a kinsman, almost a brother. After all, they both had roots in the low country. Didn't that give Hugo Van Elland a certain right of ownership? Only he, Hugo Van Elland, understood this tortured man. That's why the four sketches needed to be in his vault by Christmas, but now a wrench was thrown into the works. Van Ellen sat at his desk and pulled a rubber band from around his mail. On top of the stack was the latest overseas edition of the *Rome Daily American*, dated October 16. As he scanned the headlines and read on, his jovial mood turned dark.

Van Elland was really fuming now. He yanked a card roughly from his Rolodex and laid it on the desk blotter. He grabbed a manila envelope, stuffed the front page inside, and scribbled an address in Queens. He checked his watch to make sure he could get to the post office on Sea Road before they closed.

CHAPTER 32

THE HEADLINE

Thursday, October 26, 1967
Queens, New York

Chuck Iverson was worried. Monday the sixteenth had come and was long gone, with no word yet from that lowlife Jimmy the Blade. Van Elland had also gone radio silent. That wasn't good. Iverson was late with his delivery to Hugo, but his hands were tied. He had no idea where the spear was, or if Jimmy had even pulled off the job. He raised the garage door. A stiff October wind was blowing in across Flushing Bay. He walked to the mailbox and flipped the lid. As usual, there was a stack of junk mail addressed to the defunct taxi company that preceded him in the decrepit building. Flipping through and tossing the trash on the sidewalk, he finally hit paydirt: a manila envelope from Van Elland. Instead of cash, however, the only thing inside was the front page of an English-language newspaper from Italy. He tucked it under his arm and went back inside, pulling the corrugated tin door down behind him. He threw the paper down and put his glasses on. Then he read the headline.

STRABO SOCIETY MEMBERS DERAIL
DISFIGUREMENT OF PRICELESS ICON

Iverson took off his glasses and put his head in his hands for a full minute. Then he took a deep breath, put his glasses back on, and read the story.

Strabo, the New York–based geographic society, was involved in foiling a crime here in Rome early Sunday morning. Senior adviser Artemis Fletcher and a junior member known only by the name Olorin were instrumental in halting the desecration of a sculpture considered sacred by the faithful. The incident took place on around midnight at the Church of Santa Maria della Vittoria. A man was attempting to saw a large section from Gian Lorenzo Bernini's masterpiece The Ecstasy of Saint Teresa when the two scholars, with the aid of a baritone from the Rome Opera, accosted him, preventing the crime. The incident took place on the night before the feast of Saint Teresa, and the parish sexton remarked that the crime would have been doubly tragic on such an occasion.

According to a spokesman for the Roman police, the perpetrator was an American by the name of James Fleming. The spokesman added that he carried a duffel bag containing a passport, four hundred dollars, a return air ticket to New York, and additional papers. The spokesman declined to describe the contents of the additional papers, saying only that an investigation is still ongoing. No further information was given, except that Fleming is being held in custody by Roman authorities, awaiting trial.

Iverson closed his eyes, shutting out the world momentarily. He glanced up at the vast tin roof, as if help might be arriving from there. Then he continued reading.

Fletcher deflected credit for her role in the incident, telling the *Daily American* that the case was cracked back in New York by Sarah Lawrence College professor Arthur Bainbridge, who analyzed certain clues that led the art historians to the scene of the crime. One question remains: Was the perpetrator a lone wolf, or was he part of a conspiracy? Hopefully more will be revealed in time.

Iverson reached for his bottle of Scotch. His hand was shaking as he poured a pint glass halfway and filled the rest with Mountain Valley spring water. After a long quaff, he made a mental list of the dangers bearing down on him. It was bad enough that Van Elland would now have a target on his back. The Roman police had probably already been in touch with the FBI and the NYPD. Iverson knew the contents of those additional papers in Jimmy the Blade's duffel bag. He had written the instructions himself, right there on the desk where he was sitting.

A garbage truck rumbled past on 31st Avenue, heading for the dock where the trash barges were loaded. The noise startled Iverson, and he looked around the barn in a panic. The huge room seemed to be closing in on him. He shook it off and tried to come up with the best course of action, but a cornered rat rarely comes up with the best course of action. Iverson settled on irrational rage, muttering to himself.

"This is all the fault of that witch Fletcher. She and that pest Macduff! Now they've got Arthur Bainbridge in on the deal. Stuffy old Bainbridge? We graduated Yale together. We pledged to the Skull and Bones club on the same night. He was already a bore back then, so now he's a detective?"

Iverson started thinking fast. Escape, yes. He couldn't just sit in a garage in Queens and wait for the law to show up. But first, revenge. Revenge against Fletcher and her crew of stuffed-shirt professors. He shouted to the empty hall.

"Crimefighters? I'll show them a crime. I'll bring them down! I'll bring down Strabo!"

He paused. A brilliant idea had hatched in his panicked brain.

"That's it! I'll wipe Strabo from history, and the godforsaken Society with him!"

Now he had a plan. A plan that would fulfill his promise to Van Elland to deliver his blasted collateral, while also wiping out the very reason for the Society's existence in a single stroke. No, it would take two strokes. Two masterstrokes, and he would strike them himself.

Iverson put in a call to his fake documents man. He needed a passport and a college faculty identification card, both with the name Arthur Bainbridge. He dug into his remaining Van Elland cash to book a round trip flight to Rome, leaving New York on October thirty-first, arriving early the next morning, with a shorter flight to Paris and back, leaving Rome at noon, followed by the return flight to New York. He would explain to the travel agent that he had some urgent research to do in Europe before fall semester exams.

It was good to be planning an operation, good to be thinking big. He was the king of his castle in Queens. Preparations made, he raised his pint glass, now filled to the brim with Scotch, and called for a toast in the big, empty room, with only a few rats in attendance.

"If you want something done right…"

He intoned the words solemnly, as if they had never been uttered before.

"You've got to do it yourself!"

Chuck Iverson broke into a classic evil movie villain laugh, and his laughter echoed off the brick walls and tin doors of the old taxi barn.

CHAPTER 33

THE WRENCH IN THE WORKS

Iverson's histrionics were interrupted when the phone rang, echoing off the rusty tin roof.

"Hello? Yes, I got the newspaper story. Look, wait, wait. Before you get started, Hugo, I can explain everything. No, what I mean is, I can't explain anything. All I know is that I had a guy set up, paid, and sent to Rome. He was checked out!"

"Who checked him out, Chuck?"

"What are you talking about. I did, of course!"

Van Elland lowered his voice to a James Cagney snarl. "That's exactly the problem here, isn't it? I hired you to acquire the collateral I need to make the Van Gogh deal go forward. You're the one who insisted on that stupid spear heist. Who wants a sawed-off spear anyway?"

"How do you think I feel, Hugo? That spear means a lot to me."

"You know what means a lot to me, Chuck? My situation here! Do I have to remind you that I promised to present a piece for collateral before my contacts in Germany and California will even make a move? This is a complex deal, Chuck, a global deal. I'm kicking myself for having confidence in you when nobody else within fifty miles of Times Square would touch you with a ten-foot pole. Too much past publicity, too much ego, too much of no spear on the date promised."

"Okay, Hugo. I screwed up. No, our guy screwed up."

"Correction. Your guy."

"Just give me a chance to fix things up."

"Listen to me. The Stuttgart job is already done. We're in this. I've got a man coming to confirm that I've got the collateral before they hit the other three museums."

"Okay, look. Just give me a little time. Forget the spear. I've got something even bigger, and just to make sure we don't get double-crossed again, I'll do the job myself."

"Great. You'll do the job yourself. I can see the headline now. 'Pipe-Smoking, Tweed-Wearing Seventy-Year-Old Ex-Con Pulls Off the Heist of the Century.'"

"You know what, Hugo? You know what? You might be onto something there. You'll see. Give me a week. I've got a plan and yes, I'm pulling it off myself. I'll let you know as soon as I've got the swag, and you can come to my place here in Queens and pick it up in person."

"You're out of your mind, Chuck. Too many hours tossing a tennis ball at the wall in the Danbury pen. Let me warn you, if you don't come up with something for me to use as collateral to fund the Van Gogh jobs, you'll wish you were back in the pen. Look, I tossed your address in the trash. I've got my pen in hand. Give it to me again for the Rolodex, just in case you're thinking of welching on this job, too, and I need to send somebody to straighten things out."

"Twelve hundred 22nd Street, on the corner of 31st Avenue in Flushing. Big garage near the transfer station."

"Transfer station. You mean the dump where they load the garbage barges? Vloek! I got a guy whose office is at the dump. Great. Just great."

"Give me a little time on this, Hugo. A week. I'll make it right."

"Alright already. Don't screw up again."

The phone went dead.

CHAPTER 34

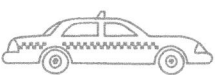

THE DOUBLE HEIST

Tuesday, October 31, and Wednesday, November 1, 1967
Queens, New York, to Rome, Paris, and back to Queens

Over the previous four days Iverson had collected the bogus passport, with his first non–mug shot photo in three years, along with his fake Sarah Lawrence faculty ID and the two sets of plane tickets. He bought an inexpensive but sharp-looking suit at E. J. Korvette along with a pair of Florsheim oxfords. A Gillette razor, a can of Barbasol, a tortoiseshell comb, and a tube of Brylcreem rounded out his toilet kit.

On the morning of Tuesday, October 31, Iverson washed up and shaved at the garage slop sink, put on his new suit, and took a cab into Forest Hills, where he purchased a briefcase. He walked two blocks to Central Art Supply, where he filled the briefcase with various items he would need for his operation. Just for practice, he smiled broadly as he walked past the cashier without paying. Iverson got a kick out of the fact that the shops along Metropolitan Avenue were bedecked with witches and jack-o'-lanterns. He had his own Halloween costume on, but his Samsonite trick bag was going to be filled with treats a whole lot more lucrative than candy corn.

At noon, he boarded a Boeing jet for the nine-hour flight direct to Rome. The 707 arrived on schedule at seven a.m. Rome time, November 1. With no checked baggage, Iverson headed straight for the train into Roma Termini. Once in Rome proper, he hailed a taxi.

"Cortile del Belvedere, *per favore*."

Ten minutes later he paid the driver and stepped onto the sacred ground of Vatican City. Pious pilgrims thronged Saint Peter's Square, hoping to be blessed by the pope on All Saints' Day, but Iverson wasn't in town looking for a benediction. He inquired in English at an information desk.

"Vatican Apostolic Library?"

The clerk, a young lay brother, smiled at the distinguished, well-dressed older man.

"*Buongiorno*! Your credentials, please"

"Of course."

Smiling, Iverson handed over his passport and fake Sarah Lawrence identification card.

"Just a few minutes, *per favore*."

The lay brother disappeared into the massive edifice.

Iverson enjoyed the Roman sun for ten minutes while he waited. He knew that someone in the building would be contacting the campus to confirm that there was indeed an Arthur Bainbridge on the faculty, and he knew that the answer would be yes.

The young man returned and handed Iverson's credentials to him.

"Professor Bainbridge, you are the author of *Icon: An Overview of 14th Century Byzantine Art*, are you not?"

"I am indeed."

"A favorite of mine. It's an honor to meet you. Researching a new book?"

"I am. I won't be long. I'm hoping to attend Mass at noon."

"I will escort you to the reading room. Wait until I tell my art history class who I admitted to the library today!"

Iverson approached the circulation desk.

"*Buongiorno*, Professor Bainbridge. I was informed that you will be doing some research with us this morning. Can you tell me exactly what you will need? We have twenty-six miles of shelves and sixty-five thousand ancient codices, so browsing is not possible."

"No problem, *signorina*."

He handed her a yellow legal sheet from Central Art Supply, on which he had written Palimpsest: Vaticanus 2306.

"Excellent! You are well prepared, professor, just as one would expect."

"Preparation does indeed expedite things."

"Here are your white gloves. Do you need privacy to examine the document?"

"That would be wonderful."

"I will show you to a private quiet room. The palimpsest will be brought to you. When you are finished, just leave it on the table and it will be refiled later in the day."

They arrived at the sound-dampening door of a small room, with a shade that could be pulled down to ensure privacy.

"I understand you are hoping to attend Mass at noon?"

"That's correct."

"We will expedite our search. Please make yourself comfortable."

As soon as the palimpsest was delivered by a young orderly, Iverson went straight to work. Wearing the white gloves, he laid his art materials on the table next to the ancient book. It had a hard parchment cover, which he was able to imitate passably well. With no time to worry about details, he took a gamble on the fact that, with sixty-five thousand of these items stored on twenty-six miles of shelves, the orderly who would pick it up later wouldn't recall the individual features of one palimpsest. He was tempted to open it, to see the interesting effect of an ancient Roman transcription of Strabo with a fifth-century passage from the New Testament written right over it, but there was no time for art appreciation. Iverson had another appointment to make. He slipped the document into a linen bag and tucked it into his bag, laid the counterfeit version on the table, and packed his art materials carefully. On the way out, he waved to the circulation librarian.

"*Grazie! Buongiorno!*"

It was nine a.m. Time to get back to the airport for his ten a.m. flight.

At eleven a.m., he was looking down at the Alps from his window in a small Dassault Falcon 20. He was feeling on top of the world himself. Jimmy the Blade was right, after all. The Vatican was the big time. And he'd done it! Chuck Iverson had hit the Vatican! And best of all, he had a piece of Strabo in the briefcase on his lap.

The Falcon touched down at Orly Airport promptly at noon. Iverson cradled his briefcase on the thirty-minute cab ride through traffic to the Imperial Library, in the heart of the city. He paid the cabbie in US dollars and stepped out into the all-encompassing artwork that is Paris.

There was no time to spend on aesthetic appreciation. He was on the tightest of schedules. Gaining access to the library's collection was simply act two of his starring role as Professor Bainbridge from Sarah Lawrence. The staffers were friendly and polite, just as they were at the Vatican, and if they telephoned the Sarah Lawrence switchboard to confirm that there was indeed an art professor on the faculty by the name of Arthur Bainbridge, they would have gotten a reassuring *certainement*.

In a matter of minutes, Iverson was seated alone in another private room, waiting for delivery of codex 1395. This was a much bigger trove than the single palimpsest in Rome. The Imperial Library held the most complete known versions of *Geographica*, dating from the Middle Ages. In an hour's time, Iverson could seize possession of the very history on which the Strabo Society was founded. Sure, they could humiliate him and pack him off to jail, but they couldn't stop him from owning their very namesake!

The door opened, and an *auxillaire* rolled in a cart stacked with a numbered set of nine volumes.

"*Merveilleux. Merci beaucoup.*"

"*De rien, professeur.*"

Iverson's timetable allowed for one hour in Paris before his return flight to Rome and from there to New York. He laid his briefcase open on the table next to the nine volumes of Parasinius 1395. That was his *gros prix*, his *coup de maitre*, his *grande victoire*. He smiled at the stack of books as if greeting a beloved family. Then he bent to his work.

Number 1395 was more than just an old book. It was a treasure trove of gorgeous medieval artwork, the pages adorned with arabesque designs and ornate capital letters setting off the Latin paragraphs. There was no time and no practical way to copy the artwork and text. Iverson stuck to his technique of molding and modifying his art materials and the blank notebooks he had carried from New York to create a replica of each volume realistic enough to pass casual inspection, as long as the real thing was not present for comparison.

In the interest of caution, he made counterfeits of volumes two through nine, banking on the prospect that an intern gathering stock for refile at the close of day would likely only glance at the top of the stack. It was a gamble, but smuggling artifacts through the Khyber Pass was a gamble, too, and he'd pulled that off years ago. Iverson felt a rush of adrenaline. After three years in prison, he was back in the saddle, pulling of the greatest heist of his career.

At 1:30 pm, he smiled at the *bibliothecaire* as he passed the circulation desk.

"*Au revoir, professeur!*"

"*Au revoir, et merci beaucoup.*"

At four p.m., Iverson was boarding a Boeing 707 for the trip back to New York. Nine hours later at JFK Terminal 1, he used his phony Bainbridge passport one last time at the US passport holders exit.

He'd pulled it off. He dialed Van Elland's number from a phone booth and left a message on the answering machine.

"Job done. Pick up the bundle in person at my place tomorrow."

CHAPTER 35

THE WEB IS SPUN

Thursday, November 2, 1967
New York City

The phone rang on Kevin Macduff's office desk.

"Strabo Society. This is Director Macduff. How may I help you?"

"Mister Macduff, this is Frank Hunter. I'm calling from FBI headquarters here in New York."

"Call me Kevin. What can I do for you, Frank?"

"We're hoping you can help us in an investigation."

"Okay. Shoot."

"We got two leads over the teletype this morning, both from Europe, and both involving old pieces of art."

"Antiquities. Go on."

"Our undercover law enforcement partners in Germany are known, to make a long name short, as the BND. They have intelligence agents planted here and there in the criminal underworld. Earlier this month one of them was contacted about pulling off an art heist in Stuttgart, at their national gallery. The BND agent agreed to take the job, and a fee was paid in American dollars. The guy doing the hiring lives on Long Island. Does the name Hugo Van Elland ring a bell?"

"Van Elland? Sure. He's one of our big donors. Old Dutch family money. I don't think he's ever worked a day in his life. Fancies himself an art collector. He's got a big spread out in Southampton. Tell me, Frank, did the job come off?"

"Well, obviously BND agents don't actually steal stuff, but she collected enough evidence through correspondence to nail Van Elland on conspiracy to commit grand larceny. She's got him convinced that she's already done the job and has the piece stashed in a warehouse in Hamburg. He expects it to show up when that new Hanseatic docks here around Christmas."

"Oh yeah. The old one burned up, right here on the waterfront last year. That was a heck of a fire."

"You got that right. Anyway, we could grab Van Elland right now on the conspiracy charge, but we've got a feeling down here at headquarters that we're looking at the tip of an iceberg. I'm going before a magistrate today to plead probable cause for a search warrant. We want to take a look at that big spread out in Southampton."

"So, what's the piece that Van Elland thinks is stashed in Hamburg?"

"Let me check my notes. Art is not my thing."

Shuffling sounds.

"Here we go. I'm reading off the report. Sketch of Langlois Bridge at Arles. I probably butchered the pronunciation."

"You did. Wow. He's not messing around. There are only four of those sketches in existence. The bridge at Arles. Van Gogh did those sketches because he was getting ready to do a painting of the bridge. That painting is one of his greatest works."

"I'll bet that bridge is a big tourist attraction now, like the Eiffel Tower."

"Actually, it was blown up during World War II."

"Whoops, that was probably my platoon!"

"I think it was the Nazis. Look, Frank, we need to act fast on this. Here's my first suggestion. Have your people get in touch with the Rhode Island School of Design, the Los Angeles County Museum, and the Morgan Library here in New York. That's where the other three sketches are. Tell them to take them off exhibit and put them under lock and key. Knowing Van Elland, he's looking at collecting the full set. When is that search warrant gonna be executed?"

"We're looking at five a.m. tomorrow, if the judge agrees tonight."

"Let me make another suggestion. I've recently become acquainted with a professor of art history out at Sarah Lawrence. He'd be an asset in evaluating whatever Van Elland has out there in his basement and outbuildings."

"Sure, if five in the morning isn't too early for him. What's his name?"

"Professor Arthur Bainbridge."

"You're kiddin' me!"

"That's his name. Professor Arthur Bainbridge."

Frank Hunter put his hand over the receiver and shouted across the office.

"Joe, you're not gonna believe this one!"

He got back on the line.

"I tell ya, it never rains around here but it pours!"

"Okay, Frank, what's Joe not gonna believe?"

"Bainbridge's name came across the wire this morning. It seems that just yesterday he pulled off a heist in Rome and another in Paris, both on the same day. Talk about a pro!"

Macduff stifled a horse laugh.

"Bainbridge! Frank, if Bainbridge is a master thief, I'm Babe Ruth."

"He was identified at the Imperial Library in Paris and, hang on to your hat for this one, the Vatican!"

Macduff sighed.

"Frank, you ever heard of a fake ID?"

"Well, I'm just giving you the info we have to go on."

"Do me a favor. Before you bang on his door with hand-cuffs and give the old man a heart attack, let me ask a few questions from sources that are more reliable than a couple of library interns. Bainbridge is friends with one of my senior advisers here at the club, Artemis…"

Hunter interrupted him. "Fletcher. Artemis Fletcher."

"You know who she is?"

"Of course I do. Who else is named Artemis?"

"How do you know about her?"

"She's a legend around headquarters. We've tracked her from Katmandu to Kyoto and back. Never stepped in to help her because she never needs any help. She's a one-woman law enforcement agency. Wasn't she involved in cracking the case of that screwball trying to saw a statue in Rome last month?"

"She was there, but it was Bainbridge who cracked the case. I'm telling you, he's one of the good guys. Let me call Artemis and have her explain to him that somebody grabbed his identity and pulled off a heist. I'm sure he's got an alibi. By the way, what got stolen in Rome and Paris?"

"I thought you'd never ask. Old books. Really old. The guy who wrote them was named Strabo. I figured that would get your attention."

Macduff nearly dropped the receiver. "Frank, I gotta go. Let's not pull old Bainbridge in on this. I'll ask Artemis to get a written alibi for you to check out, and I think we should invite her to the house party tomorrow morning at Van Elland's place. The Strabo thing is a whole different can of worms."

"All good. I gotta go, too. Hey, how about that Namath? Broadway Joe! I think the Jets are finally gonna have a winning season this year, in fact I've got money on it."

"That's great, Frank. Good luck. Look, I'm gonna make a call."

Macduff hung up, then picked up the receiver again and dialed the house in Valhalla. He got the answering machine.

"Artemis? Kevin. Look, um, where do I start? Okay, first things first. Please call Bainbridge right away and find out exactly where he was this past Saturday. If it wasn't Rome and Paris, he's off the hook. Call me back after you reach him."

Macduff pulled out a legal pad and jotted down the various threads that made up the day's news, trying to find a way to weave them together.

Strabo books stolen from Paris Museum and the Vatican. That equals Iverson.

Iverson's motivation. Make up for blown statue job. Revenge against the Society.

He stopped and digested the first few ideas. There had to be more to it, to pull off a job like the Vatican. Then he picked up his pencil again.

Fresh out of prison, Iverson is broke. He must be working for someone who funded the statue job, and he failed to deliver the goods. He needed a big win fast to wipe out his debt to Mister Big, whoever that is, or risk getting wiped out himself. But who is his sugar daddy?

If we assume that Van Elland is hoping to grab all four of the Van Gogh sketches, it's a safe bet that he's not going to do any of the jobs himself. We already know that he hired the wrong flunky in Germany, although he doesn't know that yet. What if he is Iverson's sugar daddy? They know each other from Strabo. In fact, old Hugo probably learned the trade from Sinclair, just like Iverson did when he was director, but now that he's a broke ex-con, he's Hugo's bootlicker.

The phone rang: Artemis calling back.

"Kevin, I just spoke with Professor Bainbridge. He's resting at home, watching Basil Rathbone play Sherlock Holmes. I think we may have spawned a new secret agent. By the way, he had his gall bladder removed over the weekend and was laid up all week. He was still in Westchester Med on Wednesday. It's all on record."

"Have the hospital get a copy of those records to me. I'll let Hunter at the FBI know to wipe the professor off his chalkboard."

"Are you going to tell me why Bainbridge needs an alibi?"

Macduff filled her in on the double heist in Europe. "So, Artemis, with Bainbridge cleared, Iverson is the obvious choice for our Strabo book thief."

"But how would he know about the professor?"

"Got me. Both Yale guys, the important thing right now is that apparently, he pulled off an Oscar-worthy performance as the professor over in Europe yesterday."

"So if we find Iverson, we find the stolen books."

"Correct. Look, I've been working a few things out on paper. Let me read you my notes."

Kevin filled her in on his connect-the-dots, with Iverson and Van Elland as the dots that still needed a string to connect them.

"The FBI are getting a search warrant for Van Elland's property tomorrow morning before sunrise. You and I are cleared to take part. Maybe our connecting string is out there."

"I'm in. Let's meet at Joe Junior's Diner at four a.m., near the Midtown Tunnel, and we can ride out on the expressway together."

CHAPTER 36

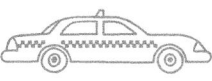

THE HOUSE PARTY

Friday, November 3, 1967
Southampton, New York

Hunter, Macduff, Artemis, and four agents dressed in black suits convened in the predawn dark at the entrance to Van Elland's estate on the shore at Southampton. Two stone pillars, each engraved with the words The Night Watch, guarded the entrance to a long gravel driveway.

Hunter was the team leader. He whispered his orders to the group.

"Burke and Ryan, let me introduce Kevin Macduff and Artemis Fletcher. Macduff has been here before."

Hunter produced a hand-drawn map of the property, pointing at it with a gloved index finger.

"Burke and Ryan, you guys take up stations at the shed and the garage. The warrant requires Van Elland to give up the keys. If he won't do it, we kick the doors in. Once we're inside the house, O'Grady and Byrne will head straight to the basement and begin the inventory. Van Elland is restricted to the main floor. I'll keep an eye on him. He's elderly, and I don't think he'll be armed."

Macduff snorted. "But one never knows, eh?"

"Well, right now everything's a guess. And there's another wild card. Dogs. He was divorced years ago and he lives alone on his rancho here. Keep your jackets and gloves on in case he's got canine watchmen."

Burke chimed in, pointing to the engraving on the stone pillars. "The night watch. Looks like he doesn't welcome visitors."

"You wouldn't either if you were hoarding twenty years' worth of stolen art. All right, that's about it. Fletcher and Macduff, I'm going to need you two to circulate around the main floor and identify stuff for the inventory. I don't know beans about art. Any questions? Good, let's go."

A cloak of silence came down as the intrepid seven passed through the unwelcoming gateposts and started up the gravel drive. They hadn't gone more than twenty paces when they heard a low, menacing growl in the darkness ahead of them. Flashlight beams revealed two sets of yellow eyes. A pair of black German Shepherds blocked the driveway, their teeth bared in a snarl.

Artemis whispered to herself.

"Ah, the night watch. And here I thought Van Elland just meant the Rembrandt painting."

She signaled for the group to freeze. Then she walked forward, directly toward the dogs. They growled again. She continued advancing. Artemis meditated on the Italian tarot card Forza d'Animo: Strength of Spirit. That was the card that had enabled her to pacify the werewolf in Amalfi. She closed her eyes and breathed deeply, showing no fear. The dogs tilted their heads and whined, inquisitive rather than threatening. They were curious why the stranger wasn't retreating.

Artemis removed her gloves and knelt a few feet in front of the dogs, searching for a channel of silent communication. Hunter threw an incredulous glance at Macduff, who shrugged. The dogs approached the kneeling figure, and she extended her hands, palms up. She held them steady and let them sniff until they were satisfied that she was not a threat. Pacified, they wandered back into the darkness to find their water bowls.

The group continued toward the house. Hunter whispered to Macduff, "What in the name of Marlin Perkins was that all about?"

Macduff shrugged again and whispered, "Heck if I know. She's got a way with animals."

Burke and Ryan split off to man their stations at the shed and garage. The other five continued onward to the front steps of the house. That's where the silence was broken. Hunter banged loudly on the door.

"FBI! Open up! We are executing a court-ordered search warrant!"

After a few minutes, the front door opened a crack, a small chain still fastened.

"No! This is a private home. You can't enter!"

"I'm sorry sir, but two judges in the Southern District of New York disagree with you. Now open up!"

"No! I will call my lawyer!"

"Fine, call him after you open the door. It's cold out here."

"No! Absolutely not! Get off my property now!"

Hunter nodded to O'Grady, a 220-pound former linebacker in his days at Fordham. He threw his full weight on the door, and it swung wide open, flinging Van Elland, in pajamas and bathrobe, backward into the foyer.

"Mr. Van Elland, I have the signed warrant here for your attorney's perusal. Please make yourself comfortable while my men…"

He glanced over at Artemis.

"I mean, while my team has a look around. Now, the keys, if you please, to the shed and the garage."

"No. They are my private property!"

"All right then. O'Grady, please go around and assist agents Burke and Ryan with those doors. Now, Mister Van Ellen…"

"Van Elland!"

"Of course, my apologies, sir. You and I will have a seat right here by the phone. You can make one call. You might advise your lawyer that your house is being searched by court order because you are a suspect in an investigation of international criminal conspiracy to commit grand larceny. Then you and I can relax for a while. Do you happen to have any coffee?"

At six a.m., after the long ride out on the Long Island Expressway, coffee did indeed seem like a good idea. Artemis didn't know if it was part of search warrant protocol to temporarily seize a couple of mugs and put a coffee pot on to boil, but Hunter was the one who had brought it up. She ran the idea by him, and he assured her that a cup of coffee had never gotten a case thrown out of court. She opened a kitchen cabinet and found the mugs, along with a blue tin can of ground coffee.

Fortified with Maxwell House, she and Macduff began surveying the main floor. True to his lineage, Van Elland definitely favored Dutch painters. Artemis felt like she was strolling through the Met. A Vermeer, a Mondrian, and could that possibly be a Bosch? If any one of them could be confirmed as hot, every piece would be carefully packed and taken into Manhattan for evaluation of its authenticity and provenance, and checked against lists of stolen museum pieces dating back to the 1940s. Some of these pieces, she thought with a shudder, might have been part of the Nazi hoard. Coffee mug in hand, she wandered into Van Elland's home office. On the desk was a calendar, a half-empty bottle of stroopwafel liqueur, a Montblanc fountain pen, and an item that stopped Artemis in her tracks. Macduff was in the kitchen. She called out to him.

"Kevin, can you come in here? Right now!"

Macduff came in and stood on the far side of the desk.

"No, stand over here next to Van Elland's chair, and look straight down."

"Holy cow."

He picked up a card, evidently torn out of the Rolodex.

"Read it out loud," Artemis said.

"Iverson, Friday morning. 1200, 122nd Street, Flushing. Corner of 31st Avenue."

"Read the rest."

Macduff read the added scrawled comment: "A dump!"

They looked at each other, momentarily stunned. Artemis spoke first.

"We found him."

"So it looks like old Hugo Van Elland is Iverson's sugar daddy. We need to get to that dump pronto. I'll copy down the address and put the Rolodex card in Hunter's hands. We're gonna need backup."

Macduff drained his coffee mug.

"Let's get moving."

CHAPTER 37

THE FOX'S DEN

The normally two-hour trip west on the expressway seemed to take forever. The morning throng of rush hour commuters was crawling toward the Midtown Tunnel, heading toward their nine-to-five cubicles in the towering skyscrapers. Artemis and Macduff weren't heading for any skyscrapers. They were looking for a dump down by the Flushing Bay waterfront, a dump that just might be housing priceless ancient books and a crook on the run.

They exited on Grand Central Parkway, crossed Flushing Creek, and took a quick exit on College Point Boulevard. A few blocks to the north, Macduff made a left on 31st Avenue, and one long block later they were at the corner of 122nd Street. To their right was a large, dilapidated building with three pull-down garage doors. Immediately in front of them, had they continued a block further on 31st Avenue, was the ramp leading into the marine transfer station. Macduff pulled over across the street from the garage doors and cut the engine.

"Holy cow, Kevin. An actual dump."

"Van Elland wasn't kidding. Looks like our old pal Iverson isn't quite living the Manhattan high life anymore."

Artemis stared fixedly out of the car's passenger window at the rundown building. A rusted sign hung halfway off its mounting hardware above the three doors. Faded letters spelled out a story of bankruptcy and abandonment:

GOTHAM TAXI

Macduff recognized Artemis's determined look. He'd seen it before, and he prepared himself for what was coming next. He knew there was no use in trying to head it off.

"Kevin, I know the NYPD are on their way, and we ought to watch and wait, but this is personal for me. Just give me a moment."

She was thinking back to being tied up on an ice sheet in the Himalayas, with vultures circling overhead, and she was thinking of being tailed around the globe by hired assassins. Iverson was the mastermind behind all of that. Even from his prison cell, he'd had a hit called on her for three years. As she stared fixedly across the street, the blowing trash turned to tumbleweeds and the dilapidated building faded, as a hazy vision began to form in her mind's eye. It was the cave from her second dream in Mexico. The old Navajo woman was completing the sand painting. Sagebrush smoke was rising from a smudge. Suddenly the woman turned, her face in shadow, silhouetted by the shaft of light behind her. She gestured to Artemis, beckoning her to enter the shadowy cave. Then she was enveloped in the sage smoke. Artemis woke from her reverie and turned to Macduff.

"I'm not waiting for the police. I'm going in."

"Artemis—"

He cut himself off.

"I'll cover for you out here. If he comes out the door, I'll nail him. The cops should be here any minute."

"That's why I've got to go in now. I want him to see me first."

CHAPTER 38

THE NEMESIS

Iverson had been running on fumes since he first boarded the jet to Europe, pulling off jobs in two cities and crossing five time zones twice, all in a single day. Back in New York, he put in a call to Van Elland and set up a meeting at the garage. Having stayed off the sauce while he did the European job, he was making up for lost time with a fresh bottle of Scotch for breakfast. Now he had the goods to wipe out his debt with the old Dutchman, and it no longer looked like he'd be fitted for concrete shoes anytime soon. Flushing Bay was a little too close for comfort, and the lovely view of Rikers Island didn't do much to calm his nerves. Today, though, he felt okay. He'd pulled off a job that would be the envy of the trade. Paris would have been big enough, but for Chrissake, the Vatican! For the first time since walking out of Danbury, Iverson felt like he was back in the game.

There was a loud knock on the middle garage door. Iverson picked up the briefcase packed with the Strabo manuscripts. It would be a pleasure to hand it off to Van Elland, in exchange for his next infusion of cash.

"Hang on, Hugo! I'll be right there! You'll be very happy!"

He rolled up the door and stared in disbelief, too shocked to react to what he saw. It was impossible.

"Good morning, Chuck! What ya got there in the briefcase, some old books, maybe?"

He couldn't put Artemis and his garage hideout together in the same mental picture, but there she was. She, who brought down Doyle's helicopter singlehandedly, then tracked Doyle to Japan, where she hogtied him in a temple. She was standing in front of him, and he was all alone, defenseless. He realized how terrified he was of her.

He pushed her out of his way and ran toward 31st Street, but a man jumped out of a parked car and tackled him to the sidewalk. He wrenched his way free, dropping the briefcase. He could hear sirens coming from all sides. Iverson bolted out onto the street. A garbage truck was rumbling slowly past, slow enough for him to grab onto a steel bar with both hands and hold on for dear life, for dear freedom. He glanced back just long enough to recognize the man who had tackled him. It was Macduff, his own successor as director of Strabo. Iverson's mind was reeling as the truck pulled into the darkness of the transfer shed.

The garbage truck ground to a halt at the waterside. Unloading was automated, so no sanitation men were around. The driver, unaware of his passenger, initiated the hydraulic dump, using a joystick to lift the entire back of the truck and open the massive tailgate, spilling the contents down into a waiting barge. Iverson was spilled along with the load, drowning in a sea of trash, the detritus of life across a swath of Queens: College Point, Corona, Jackson Heights, even the wastebins at LaGuardia. He was being crushed by garbage. As he fought his way toward the surface, he felt the barge lurch out onto Flushing Bay. He was filled with an insane rush of hope. Maybe he could get to the top and leap into the bay, swim to shore at the airport, and fly far, far away from Fletcher and her cohort of tormentors!

Iverson broke through to the surface of his trash graveyard just as NYPD police boats surrounded the barge and signaled for the tugboat pilot to heave-to. They were just offshore of Rikers Island.

PART FIVE

Passing the Torch

CHAPTER 39

THE DECISION

Thursday, November 23, 1967
Valhalla, New York

Artemis, Macduff, Tunde, and Olorin were gathered around the big table at Atalanta. Christmas decorations were already showing up all over Westchester. As the days grew short, the early sundown imposed a kind of seasonal peace on the bucolic county.

Ayotunde and Olorin had teamed up to prepare Thanksgiving dinner: a traditional Nigerian jollof rice, and a pot of after-dinner peppermint tea was steeping. The group settled into that moment of quiet satisfaction that comes after a hearty meal. Macduff was the first to break the spell.

"I've got to say, it's been a heck of a year. Three years ago, I wondered what Iverson would do when his sentence was up, and now I know. He screwed up again, and this time he's going away for a long time."

Ayotunde chuckled.

"Artemis, if you were Sherlock Holmes, Iverson played the role of Professor Moriarty."

"No! I can't be Sherlock Holmes! Kevin already dubbed Professor Bainbridge Sherlock Holmes."

"Well then you can be Miss Marple!"

"Please, I'm not that old yet!"

Artemis's mood turned pensive.

"Speaking of age, I've been doing a lot of thinking. I've been on the go since I was a kid competing in the archery contest in Japan. Then there was college, grad school, and teaching, and somewhere along the line I picked up this other life outside the classroom, roaming around the globe on secret missions like a Hollywood femme fatale. It's been an amazing whirlwind, like a tornado blowing me down various yellow brick roads, but I've come to the conclusion that global crimefighting is a young woman's game. I'm thirty-three, and I don't want to be tied to the dynamite anymore. I've been offered emeritus status at Sarah Lawrence, so I'll be able to lecture when I have something to say, but I won't be bound to the classroom. I'm going to accept, and I'm feeling like…"

She paused, a little choked up but determined to go on.

"I'm feeling like it's a good time to retire from my career as a secret agent."

The group was silent, waiting for her to finish voicing her thoughts.

"Tunde and Olorin, you two have grown so quickly into brilliant agents, and you've already rescued me from tight situations. My dream now is to relax back here at my beautiful home and garden and hear all about your exploits when you get back from exotic places."

Macduff was ready with his response.

"Artemis, none of us will argue that you haven't done enough to save priceless art all around the world. I'd even go so far as to say you've saved lives as well, by making sure that dangerous criminals like Iverson, Tom Doyle, Calico Jack, and that crazy Irish professor were locked up. You've earned your retirement, and if you are nominating Tunde and Olorin as your successors in that adventure, I heartily endorse the idea. In fact, I have a couple of upcoming missions already in mind for them."

Tunde glanced with a smile at Olorin, and then turned to salute Macduff, addressing him in an air of mock formality.

"We accept, sir. Put us to work!"

Macduff raised his teacup to propose a toast.

"Congratulations and encouragement to the new crime-busting team."

They clinked glasses all around.

"Artemis, I have one more assignment for you, but that can wait until tomorrow."

CHAPTER 40

THE LAST ASSIGNMENT

Friday, November 24, 1967
Tarrytown, New York

Over ham and tomato wedges at Malandrino's Deli, Macduff outlined an unusual last mission.

"Artemis, I know I've said this before, but this is the right time to say it again. It's because of you that the Strabo Society turned around and got back on track. The administration before me were competent men, but they were as dishonest as the day is long."

"Kevin, I think back to the moment when Wulver came out of the woods and materialized at the Strabo gala, when he knew the moon was full and he would be in full wolverine mode. The entire city of New York was in hot pursuit, but all he wanted to do was live his life. He was such an idealist that I don't think he ever imagined the hatred that would rain down on him simply because he went back to a state of nature for three days a month. So-called civilized people couldn't accept that."

"And you, Artemis, had the courage to stand by him. That got you pursued halfway around the world by hired assassins."

Artemis laughed ruefully.

"Yeah, there was that."

"But you had the smarts to outwit them and the resolution to stand up to them. I saw you knock on Iverson's door, when you knew he had spent years trying to eliminate you. That moment was a life-changing goal for you."

"I was a thorn in his side, that's for sure. But it was all in a day's work."

"It was more than that, but okay now, the assignment. It's a bit different. It's a training session."

"Think back, way back to last night. I'm retiring, remember?"

"That's just it." He sighed. "Artemis, there's a lot more to the Strabo Society than collecting art and exploring exotic lands."

"Sure, there's education, scientific research, publication of papers..."

"A lot more than that. More than I am at liberty to spell out."

He chose his words carefully.

"This organization is part of something worldwide. To be an initiate requires training, but to become a retiree requires a certain kind of training, a higher training, as well."

"I was recruited because of my crossbow skill and knowledge of world history, right?"

"That was part of it, to be sure. A large part."

"That and what else?"

"Your father, Alcon Fletcher, and your mother, Demeter Chthonia, began your training before you were born, and that training has continued right up to the present moment."

"I never met my mother. She died when I was born."

"Of course. But they had done a ceremony called the bless-ingway when you were still in Demeter's womb. The ceremony confirmed that you would follow this path, the path of service, and that you would leave the world a better place when you finished this part of your journey."

"How do you know all of this? You're my age!"

"I am, but as the director of the Strabo Society, I've been initiated myself into higher knowledge, access to records. Your parents were very high up in a global fellowship. Strabo is only a small part. You've played an important role, and your upcoming retirement is actually an initiation to a higher level of service."

He sipped his coffee.

"That's all I can tell you. Trying to explain further in words would accomplish nothing."

This time he finished his coffee and set the cup down.

"Here is your flight reservation to Phoenix for tomorrow. You will be met by a friend of the Society. His name is Atsa. No crossbow needed."

Kevin stood up and reached out his hand. They shook, and he held her hand for a few extra heartbeats.

"Artemis, working with you has been great, but simply knowing you has been one of the finest things in my life. Thank you for everything."

He left five dollars on the table, put his hat on, and got up to leave. He turned back at the café door.

"And we will meet again."

EPILOGUE

APOTHEOSIS

Saturday, November 25, 1967
Phoenix, Arizona

Atsa, a young Navajo man, met Artemis at the arrivals gate.

"If you have no checked bags, Miss Fletcher, we can depart immediately."

"No checked bags, just my trusty duffel. Kevin wasn't clear on how long this mission might take."

"It won't take long, Miss Fletcher. In fact, it will be over by daylight tomorrow."

"It will be good to get back home. And please, call me Artemis."

"Of course, Artemis. It's always good to get back home."

"Atsa. Is that a Navajo name drawn from nature?"

"That's correct. It means 'eagle.'"

"Ah. A high-flying bird."

"Because the eagle flies so high, we consider it the creature that links our world with the spirit world and transports us there."

He tossed her duffel bag in the back of a Ford Bronco.

"Well, Atsa. It looks like we're going to the spirit world in a Ford pickup!"

Atsa didn't laugh.

"There are many ways to get there, Miss Fletcher—um, Artemis."

Artemis could see that Atsa was a young man of a serious nature. She decided against further quips.

He turned north on Highway 17, rising into the high desert. They passed the monumental red rocks around Sedona, formations that she had hiked many times: Bell Rock, Kachina Woman, and the cliffs enclosing Boynton Canyon. Then they slowly wound their way up the switchbacks of Oak Creek Canyon, climbing higher and higher, reaching toward the Coconino Plateau.

At Flagstaff they crossed Route 66 and stopped on Highway 89 to fill the truck with gas before heading north into the Navajo Nation. The aspen and sycamore along the creek gave way to bristlecone and ponderosa pine as they passed over the foothills of the San Francisco Peaks, and then those gave way to mesquite and sagebrush. After two hours of driving on the western edge of the Painted Desert, they stopped again for gas and water at the Cameron Trading Post, where Highway 64 splits west to the Grand Canyon. They continued north on 89. Just south of Lake Powell and the Utah border, Atsa took a right-hand cutoff that headed east, deep into Navajo land.

"Tell me, Atsa. Are we heading for Horseshoe Bend?"

"Near there. Have you been to that place?"

"Years ago, on a Strabo mission for the Nation. In the interest of protecting and preserving art and antiquities, we have a long-standing relationship with the Navajo people."

"You are known here by reputation. In fact, you have fans, as you would say, of your archery here in the Nation."

"Well, my archery skills are more along the lines of the Middle Ages rather than the culture of the Southwest."

She grimaced at herself for making another quip.

They rode silently for another ten miles, then Atsa turned south for two miles and pulled the Bronco off the dirt road at what appeared to be another patch of barren desert between two formations of Navajo sandstone. They sat silently for a few minutes until a woman dressed in a calico skirt and blouse, a turquoise necklace, and silver bracelets suddenly rose out of the earth.

"Welcome, Artemis! Welcome!"

She walked to the truck, reached through the open passenger window, and took Artemis's hands, both of them. She held them for longer than a typical handshake, as if feeling for the pulse inside the younger woman's skin.

"We are honored that you are here. You have been invaluable to the Society. You have saved works of art, and more importantly, you have saved lives. You have earned a celebration."

"So, is this a surprise retirement party?"

"We don't say retirement, dear one. We say transition. Now, come with me, Artemis. Atsa, you wait for me here."

They walked over to where the woman had appeared to rise out of the ground. There was a narrow crack in the earth, only a few feet wide. From Artemis's viewpoint on the surface, it was impossible to see how deep it was. In the shade of a rock formation, a kit fox was sleeping, looking very much like a housecat with oversized ears. The sleeping animal gave Artemis a sense of comfort in the unfamiliar surroundings.

"Welcome to Owl Canyon. We are standing over the dry bed of Antelope Creek. Owl, Rattlesnake, and Antelope Canyons have been carved by this small creek. They are sacred spaces, ceremonial spaces. Outsiders are not often brought here, but you have proven yourself one of the righteous ones. This is a place of solemn ceremony, a place of transition. Now, follow me, Artemis. No problem with ladders?"

"Thank you for asking. I survived a falling rope bridge in the Himalayas. I guess I can make it down a ladder."

The ladder was steep and rickety, but Artemis's curiosity had overcome any trepidation. She climbed down facing the sheer rock wall, so it was only at the bottom when she turned around that she got a full view of the interior of the canyon. It took her breath away.

Sunlight streamed in bold rays through sandstone particles wafting up from the floor as the cool slot canyon reacted to the late afternoon heat above. The red sandstone walls, striated from eons of sporadic flash floods, emitted a glow that seemed not of this earth. Artemis felt weak in the knees, the way she felt when she first climbed the narrow stairs to Sainte-Chapelle in Paris and found herself bathed in a sea of stained-glass light. That space, however, was created by a king. This cathedral was the work of nature; the slow, steady work of water over tens of thousands of years. It was unlike any environment she had ever seen. She felt humbled. If this was a ceremony, it was in an auspicious place, and she knew where she was. She had been there before, in the second dream in Mexico. She felt no unease. Her guide introduced herself.

"I am Hawkchaser. For the first part of the ceremony, I will be the talker. Only one person talks, because we are addressing the spirit world, and we want to be clear in our expression. When I am gone, only the *hata'a'lee* will talk. Now, follow me."

The shadows in the canyon were growing long as the sunlight shifted to a slant from the west, creating new and fantastical sculptural shapes as the afternoon grew longer. They rounded an outcrop of rock and entered a sort of chamber.

"This space, Artemis, is like the hogan where we perform rituals above ground. If you look up, you will see a natural smoke hole that opens to the surface. This is *iikaah*, the place where the spirits can be contacted. Please have a seat while the *hata'a'lee* prepares the dry painting."

A blanket was spread on the floor of the canyon for Artemis to sit on. In the center of the chamber, an old woman was gazing at the canyon floor. She was making a sand painting. Her pigments were laid out next to her on a blanket: lupine for blue, wolfberry for red, tamarisk for pink, verbena for purple, and marigold for yellow. She began by using her vegetable ingredients to paint a circle in the sand, then added an arrow, two sunflower stalks, feathers outside the circle at the four wind directions, and a shield for protection. She began chanting softly, while she gently touched each symbol, and then touched the ground outside the circle, blessing the earth. She beckoned for Artemis to approach and sit closer.

Five miles up the canyon, above the Antelope Creek dry basin, a thunderhead was forming.

Hawkchaser disappeared back up the rickety ladder, and the *hata'a'lee* repeated her cycle of touching each symbol, this time touching Artemis on the knee every time in a blessing. Her head was always down, looking at the painting on the sand, and she sometimes swayed as if in a trance. Darkness was falling aboveground as she lit a sagebrush smudge. The smoke curled upward toward the narrow opening.

Five miles east on a high ridge, the Antelope Creek basin was filling with rainwater, although no rain had fallen on Owl Canyon.

A sudden downdraft of wind filled the chamber with sagebrush smoke. The *hata'a'lee* finally raised her head and fixed her gaze on Artemis. She spoke, in English.

"Artemis, I am Demeter, your mother, your creatrix. Just as you lived within me, I have also lived within you. I have cherished you as my own flesh and blood, and I have counseled and protected you, as Sky Woman, Hamsa, Kumari Devi, Kannon, and yes, as your sister Viviana Villalobos. You have grown into one of the righteous ones. You have earned your place among us. My final lesson to you is this. All the forms in which I appeared to you were really you, counseling yourself. The old ones were always within you, and now you join us. You have earned your place, and you still have much to do."

Five miles east on the high ridge, the Antelope Creek natural basin filled to the brim, and the sandy pond walls collapsed, disgorging a torrent of stormwater, mud, and rocks down the dry creek bed.

As smoke filled the chamber, Artemis's eyes half closed, and she saw her mother Demeter change shape: change into the feathered woman in the tower, the creator of the birds, wielding the paintbrush. Artemis felt herself grow smaller and smaller, down to cellular level, down to atoms, down to colors on the easel. The thunderous torrent bore down, but it went unheard, and just before it smashed into the slot canyon, Demeter, her mother and creatrix of the birds, raised her head and said, "You should know that there is another dreamer, dreaming us."

Her head dropped again, and then raised as she spoke for the final time.

"Your training is complete."

Demeter disappeared into the cloud of sagebrush smoke.

The roaring torrent rushed in, carrying Artemis up through the smoke hole to the surface. She shook the water off her wings and flew to a twisted juniper tree, where she roosted in a deep sleep. She dreamed of a long, long journey.

When she woke, it was early evening. She was gliding over a broad lake, riding a thermal current. Tall white pines cast their shadows over darkening water.

She saw two men in a canoe. She could hear them talking. One of them spoke softly about the transmigration of souls, the passage of the spirit from human to animal. The other man began shouting angrily. They drifted close to the shore, too close, lurching roughly over a fallen log. A backpack snagged on a dead branch. It rose above the canoe momentarily and then fell back into the craft. There was a bright flash on the keel of the canoe. She knew what it was. Hecatolite. Moonstone. A spearhead.

The canoe approached shore, preparing to put in, when one man struck the other with his paddle, pitching him into the shallow water. Perched in a tall white pine, delving with blazing yellow eyes, the binocular eyes of a great horned bird, and listening with ears that can hear a mouse's heartbeat deep under a snowbank, she pierced into each man's soul as she spread her broad wings and descended toward the canoe. Her first mission was to save the hecatolite spearhead.

She flexed her razor-sharp claws as she accelerated downward, focused on the moonstone.